Call It Tender

JOHN SAUL was born in Liverpool, England. For most of the year he lives in Germany, where he works as a translator. He has also lived in France, Canada and Ecuador, where he began writing fiction. He is the author of two novels, *Heron and Quin* and *Finistère*.

Also by John Saul

Heron and Quin (Aidan Ellis, 1990)
Finistère (Hopscotch, 2005)

Call It Tender

John Saul

SALT

CAMBRIDGE

PUBLISHED BY SALT PUBLISHING
PO Box 937, Great Wilbraham, Cambridge PDO CB21 5JX United Kingdom

© John Saul, 2007

First published 2007

Printed and bound in the United Kingdom by Lightning Source

Typeset in Swift 9.5/13

ISBN-13 978 1 84471 322 6 paperback

Salt Publishing Ltd gratefully acknowledges
the financial assistance of Arts Council England

1 3 5 7 9 8 6 4 2

To Dominique

Contents

Acknowledgements

I would like to thank the editors of the following publications where these stories first appeared. "G3,5" was first published in *Ambit*, "Sisters" and "Shingle Street" in *Westerly*, "History" in *Island* and "Untitled" in *Grain*.

I would also like to thank my most excellent reader, Stella Chapman.

G3,5

A hanging; evenings on the sofa; a twenty-minute plane ride.

Tradition says start with the hanging.

One snowy day in December 1976, in Erie county, western New York, as Rod Stewart topped the Billboard Hot 100 with *Tonight's the Night*, Megan Mattysek kicked away a chair beside the staircase of her home in Lotus Point, twisted once or twice (it's guessed), lost consciousness (almost certainly) and, no longer spinning, her stockinged toes brushing the carpet, suffocated to death. She was found not, as she had envisaged, by her husband Ernst—though missing his wallet, he stuck to his resolve to leave the US with son Tony immediately without returning for it—but by her nine-year-old daughter Kristin.

Open a door: mother dead; father gone; brother gone.

No wonder Kristin needs something to hold onto, a place, a home, a man. No wonder she is a lover of certainties, structure, grids. Pleased at the straight county lines in her childhood home, at the clever street system of the Mannheimer Quadrate; that we take each other always strictly within the rectangle of our bed.

But chronology says move on, swiftly.

Kristin abruptly dropped her helicopter pilot career in the US navy to come to Europe to search for her father Ernst, her long-lost brother Tony. Once located, they were strangers, not anxious to be found. Now Kristin flies a Beaver de Havilland seaplane off the Rhine and over Mannheim, pointing out the water tower and arranging souvenir photos of people's homes in streets named by numbers in the ancient grid system below. She dips a white wing and there it is, a giant waffle-iron with 144 indentations and a ringroad running like syrup round the edges, between the river Neckar and the Rhine. We have one of these photos in the living room.

We live together at G3,5, Mannheim.

It is well worth grappling with Kristin on our sofa. It stops her looking at the old film—rather a five-minute video patched together to save flaky film before it crumbled away altogether—where her mother Megan, advanced in pregnancy, holds court on her porch at Lotus Point and Ernst stands around, decidedly unrelaxed. Suddenly a tall blonde woman reaches across, her shoulders blocking the scene, before lurching back out of view. The camera pans past a tree trunk and Kristin aged seven and sweet-faced, big black curls, legs skinny as Olive Oil, enters the frame at a run. Wearing a princess's dress she's a princess with no power, finding it hard to edge between adults to get a piece of dark (must be chocolate) cake. After a hurried close-up on her father grimacing, she can be seen comically hobbledy-walking across the lawn with a piece on a plate. Acetate flickering, the camera jolts from a pair of big male shoes to sky with a corner of roof. There's a sudden shot down an empty garden, smoky trees in the distance. Next comes princess Kristin smiling her perfect smile (the smile that sheds light, that draws me to her constantly), impishly balancing some cake on the back of her hand. She appears to be told off for laying the empty plate on the bonnet of a Lincoln car (close-up on the name) parked in the driveway. Her father wags his finger but it is obviously no longer a serious scene but a re-run for the camera. Kristin runs back to the grass and does a cartwheel but the film stops with her legs and curls blurred in mid-air.

That's all.

Kristin is much less fun after watching the film. Quips are out of order. The smile fails to flash. Whatever book she has (currently Mao Zedong, biography, fifty pages in) she leaves aside for the day. We hash and rehash her father and mother and the day in '76. The video is a well-meant gift, says Kristin, but a cruel gift; there is no one left alive to go through the pictures with. Ernst died recently a millionaire with a mansion and a piece of forest above Heidelberg, leaving his daughter next to nothing—the legal minimum. But her brother Anton sent the film, pieced together from spools and cassettes found in the mansion cellar. Now Kristin, waking herself in the night, dreams of entering the house ("mom?") carefully holding a snowflake on the back of her glove, like a ladybird, ready to show; to come up against her mother noosed to the banisters.

While enduring the pain of abandonment every time she runs the video, Kristin is struggling to decipher it. Wasn't that blonde woman Mrs Dellapenta? Was her father having an affair with her? Why did he turn against her mother so? Was this reason enough to abscond with her brother to Europe?

Kristin's young self goes on her hobbledly walk. It must have been the fiftieth rehash. I took a few nuts from the bowl.

Must everything be pieced together? I found myself saying. Who did what when exactly, why exactly. Maybe you can't home in on some perfect explanation. Not everything is like a plane with a target.

Helicopters, said Kristin absorbed by the action on-screen. They were helicopters, not planes.

The past is not a set of stories, I challenged her; wishing she would stop beating herself this way.

What is it then? said Kristin.

This drove me into new territory. I regretted not having grappled straight after the eight o'clock news. Already, somewhere, I had gone badly wrong in this conversation. I looked at Kristin in her lumpy old sweater (what happened to the fun pink and peppermint T-shirts), then back at the screen. There's one certainty: that car is a Lincoln.

What is it then? Kristin repeated.

What is it? I don't think it *is* anything.

So it's a waste of time?

Her sweater was rips and holes, brown grains of coffee smudged where her irresistible sexual self used to be. Princess Kristin runs into her cartwheel.

Kristin zapped the video off. The TV came on. I pulled at a loose thread on her sweater. I had a dark feeling everything was changing for us: our bodies, our minds, how things were between us.

When Mao was a student, Kristin said taking my hand from her sweater, he lived through a freezing winter with three other students and they had one coat between them.

We're getting nowhere, I thought sighing.

I'm going to see Ludwig, I declared.

Ludwig?

Dark horses with shining flanks thundered across the screen.

I told you about Ludwig, I said. You've forgotten. He wants me to organise his birthday. I'll be gone a while. He lives at L10,1.

Kristin stared at the pictures and said, I love seeing horses cross the screen.

I know. You've told me many times.

Clint Eastwood spoke German, put a spoon in some beans.

Nick, come back soon.

We do know her family has a suicidal streak, a possible genetic disposition, but Kristin is not thought to have inherited this. No way, she says if I question her.

Little as I knew Ludwig, I found myself telling him this. I told him about the video too, the cake, the car, Mrs Dellapenta. His face up close, he listened nodding, saying yes, saying 'that's interesting'. Now I'm going to say something, he said. He pulled his hat even further down over his eyes. Apart from at work Ludwig wears a dusty black hat like a cowboy's over his eyes, indoors or out.

While her mother Megan loved her children, he said in a bumpy English, she will not have had these in her mind uppermost, or at all, at the decisive moment. So Ludwig said, and he is a doctor.

I don't see a trace of a similar attitude in Kristin, I repeated, she's too community-minded.

That's important, said Ludwig finally, that's the main point.

At any given moment, he told me, there is a main point. To grasp and hold onto.

The night had moved on, and we moved on to the business of arranging his birthday. The food, drink, music. He gave me a list of the equipment his band had to have. I told him I saw no problems.

Do you just organise, he asked close up again, or do you have an interest in music?

I organise—I said, looking aside at all the guitars and guitar cases; Ludwig had a wall of guitars at L10,1—but I wouldn't mind learning the guitar. Do you just play acoustic guitars?

I do, he said pulling his hat down as far as it could possibly go. The rest are a waste of money.

Hm, I replied. I felt the brim of his hat close to my forehead. It was getting very intense with Ludwig. The closeness was getting challenging. I recalled never having seen Ludwig with a woman. Of a sudden I longed for Kristin.

Do you . . . do you play with a pick? Or with your fingers?

That's a non-question too. I use a soft plectrum, like this.

He backed away to reach in his pocket. He showed me his plectrum.

Now for some beer, he said as if to an invisible servant.

I took a night bus from L10 to G5 and walked the rest. Past the chemist's (G4,8), a bank (G4,7): the block system of the Mannheimer Quadrate (so Kristin says to her out-of-town passengers) may sound futuristic, but predates Manhattan by more than two centuries. Otherwise (G4,4) I have been drinking a good deal of beer and, otherwise, people have always taken their own lives and otherwise other people have always been left to deal with the aftermath—themselves and the people they love and questions that cannot be answered. Otherwise (every shop has long closed; people I can't see are shouting by the bar on the corner where Kristin and I never go) there is probably always a Ludwig or someone talking about the main thing, or someone similar to him with ideas similar to his, Joni Mitchell saying we are stardust, that's the main thing, Milan Kundera reselling the idea we are poised, as Shakespeare already put down, between something and nothing, we can choose for a short short while. Past the bakery, the hairdresser's, the newsagent's— we can pin these down with details but the only significant truth, the main point now, is that Kristin needs me to catch her and hold her as she goes through this free fall set in spin by her father.

G3,7,6,5. Door to the flat.

So it's up to me now. Quietly.

Clothes off.

Kristin, you're awake? We must be well into tomorrow.

Nick, her voice from the pillow murmured: there's no point.

There is. The point is, the main point is we're here. We love each other.

We do?

We do.

How come you can speak for me?

What kind of a question is that?

A sleepy one. There's no point.

In what?

The past is past I've decided, she said in the dark. Nothing to learn from.

Yes, I said clawing, groping to combine drunkenness with affirmation, yes. There must be things. If there are things I've learned from the past they are . . . I'll tell you them tomorrow.

Why can't I sleep, she said punching the duvet. *Goddamn it.*

What?

Go to sleep.

Wait. If I've learned two things they are: 1 take the initiative; 2 never buy cheap cling-wrap.

I don't want your jokes now. Besides, you never buy *any* cling-wrap.

I'll buy some tomorrow.

OK, good.

She turned away. She slept without moving.

Days; weeks. Every night, the film. Kristin left Mao unfinished, bookmarked up a remote mountain at Dajing, having retreated from Maoping, having before that retreated from Ciping, backing up from a town to a village to a hamlet. Backtracking: I knew the feeling. Already, Kristin had stopped touching me when she passed, stopped calling me great, stopped calling me special and instead settled for saying I was unique. I didn't care for this turn from passionate to neutral. Not wanting the same fate as Mao, I sought the main point and took this to be: keep listening. I resolved to watch the video and listen to her if we watched it for ever. Weeks became more weeks. We ate, slept, we went to work, the pilot and the organiser of events. Kristin had moods, but I followed her into them. We stopped eating breakfasts, for instance. We put all the pictures we had in proper frames. We watched Megan hold court, the woman bend across; saw the shoes and the smoky trees, the plate and the car and the smile. At his birthday Ludwig sang *Gimme Some Lovin'* and *I Can See Clearly Now* and ate at a table with his hat on. Meanwhile Kristin left Mao marooned under a pile of newspapers but at least moved on, to Rosa Luxemburg (put aside), Joan Didion (aside), Matisse. We took off, circled, landed, organised. The photo business (the true profit from the flights) boomed. The action stopped mid-cartwheel.

I can't do that now.

I'm listening.

I just can't.

Is that all?

All. The main thing, as your friend Ludwig would say. My body's changed, I haven't the confidence. How come he never comes here? I don't go for this main-thing theory.

Kristin reached for her book on Matisse and stroked my cheek.

Bring Ludwig here and when he says it's the main thing that matters I shall tell him it's not.

It's not?

Matisse said: when drawing a tree, pay attention to the spaces between the leaves.

She was wearing her jacket with the green sequins.
We grappled.

The white De Havilland bobbed at its mooring, all struts and
ailerons and preening blue graphics.

You don't have to fly, Nick. You can wait in the café and
watch.

Why do that, Nick? said Ludwig. You'd be crazy. *Sag mal*
Kristin, how did you ever get into a thing like this?

Perfect eyesight.

Kristin—like crystal.

If you like. Fast reaction times. I got the idea at school. I like
speed. Power. Precision too.

Ludwig pulled his hat tight. *Wunderbar.*

So Nick, what's it going to be? How come you've never been
up with me before? I mean, what's *wrong* with you, *goddamn it*?
Look at it, it's a wonderful day, what more do you want?

OK, I'm there. You, Ludwig?

Of course, for this I'm here. And I want a photo.

Get in. Shut the door and belts on.

It has one engine? Is it Pratt and Whitney?

It is. Three-blade Hartzell propeller, main tank 95 litres, addi-
tional 75-litre tanks in the wingtips, Avgas 100LL fuel. Your belts
on? Anything else you want to know?

No, said Ludwig. That was the main thing. It's loud.

That's nothing. Wait till we stop taxiing.

What?

Of course it's *loud*, it's an old plane. Put on the headphones.

OK.

You OK?

OK. One propeller you say.

Obviously.

That's better.

What is?

With the headphones.

Check. Check.

What?

Talking to myself. Last checks.

I like it. You Ludwig?

Nick, I *love* it.

Old plane. How old?

'62. Here we go.

Ah.

All right.

Na klar.

Already a low barge is edging along below. A glint of sun slams at us, a bar of light off the river.

At a height of six hundred metres the wing straightens out, broad and true. We feel fat and confident astride the air. Kristin dips the wing and somewhere below are L10,1 and G3,5, between the Neckar and the Rhine.

Alice Balancing

They say I was clever to have painted the Alice figure. I used my daughter Francesca. She knows I have great powers; she has inherited many of them herself. I put into the picture many of the things I've gathered and treasured over the years, which is why the bookcase behind her has mikado sticks, charts crumpled and creased, puzzles, a paperweight and a bright toucan made of clay, a book titled Egypt and a jam jar simply labelled orange marmalade and not, as some would like, something strange and unlikely, such as Murano glass or Hotel de Ville. There are feathers, vials, bones, keys, a box marked Cairo. There are leaves in the air and no ground beneath her feet because she is falling. A blue urn descends through the picture with her. Nonetheless this Alice has her legs astride and firm, her gaze is unflinching, and the way she holds out one arm and the other up, with a wand with coloured streamers, makes her message clear: I am conducting the affairs of the world.

The powers she has exceed even mine. They enable her to see many miles beyond the centre of Devizes. She can see big Pete, for example, training his video camera on a plaque in front of Silbury hill. He is thinking about Daria and imagining them both on a sofa looking at this plaque and reading it. He is asking himself if Daria will want him again. But my Alice figure, whom I may as well call Alice, if my daughter Francesca doesn't mind, will not have Daria love Pete. She ordains that big Pete will keep seeing Daria but Daria will not change her mind. A torture, which has nothing to do with what he deserves or does not deserve.

They say my depiction of her silken blue dress, the simple red shoes and long white socks, her pale complexion and pale blue eyes, can be compared to works by Piero della Francesca. Rightly. This is why my daughter was christened with that name.

Big Pete stumbled awkwardly there and almost fell. He was caught up with the viewfinder and not watching the ground. His friend Maurice is eating a sandwich from the greaseproof paper bags the two of them have put on the car roof. He shows Maurice how to work the camera.

They say I am prone to moods and changes of mind, and I will prove them right, as I'm not happy to call my creation Alice. Francesca, as I will call her if my daughter doesn't mind, decrees the wind will blow an empty bag towards the field and Maurice will chase it for a hundred yards, wait, she has relented to make that ten yards. Enough to put Maurice in front of the field and see the perfect undulations, the perfect furrows in the perfect earth, the lone tree in the distance that is perfection itself.

This sight will persuade him he is right to explore natural materials, it's a turning point. He will start a late career sculpting different woods.

That is just beautiful, Maurice says to big Pete.

It is, says Pete.

Can you get it on film? That tree way over there, for instance.

Hardly. The distances are confusing for the camera.

That's a shame.

I'll try it just the same. Since you're a friend of mine.

As they clear up their picnic it seems their minds are blank. Francesca is not pleased at this lack of life. She has to do something or gets restless. She has this from me, they say. No signals from the car park. But the car is backing up. The butterfly in my Alice picture, there on the right of the bookcase, signifies it is permissible to turn to something else for a second. Francesca's favourite butterflying move is to go back and forth in time. She moves herself forward to the age of nineteen where she is painted once again, adopting the pseudonym Faraway. They say I'm not clever to use such names but this is the name she wants. I would have preferred Marianne. Or if an F had to be used, Francine, Freya. She takes off her shirt and puts on a hat with flowers round it. Her shoulders are strong. The hat covers her eyes. Hides her blonde hair, although it is still fine and straight. Her lips, her chin and her unflinchingness alone verify this is the same person.

I set one rule, the thirty-year rule, for fear she might be disappointed. She may move forward no more than thirty years.

The vision of Pete and the car has turned hazy, it's a pity there aren't more spies in the world. But the car is leaving the Silbury hill car park, going west towards Somerset. Some music is playing inside it. Maurice wants to hear Jackson Browne, because he and Jackson Browne are almost exactly the same age, a week separates them, but Francesca is not having this, she wants Tangled Up in Blue by Bob Dylan and they motor along listening to Tangled Up in Blue by Bob Dylan.

Francesca likes blue a great deal, but has yet to see bougainvillea. I'll be painting this once I have it mastered.

Big Pete is driving. A traffic report cuts out the music but Francesca cuts out the traffic report. She can't hear exactly what they're saying, but Maurice has asked about Daria.

Francesca looks into Maurice's head to see what he thinks of Daria. He thinks Daria is quite amusing. Daria tries to suntan and it doesn't work. Her legs get orange blotches which are really offputting.

She looks again to see what his take is on the question of Pete and Daria.

Maurice strokes his beard and thinks. Daria is Pete's only option. No one else is in sight for him. She will never have him again in bed. He will just torture himself with false hopes. But there is no obvious alternative.

She looks in Pete's head.

Daria is his only option. No one else is in sight. She will never have him again, in bed. He will just torture himself with false hopes. But there is no obvious way out.

Francesca stretches out her arm to detect if Daria herself is within range. She is not. Where is Daria? She persuades Pete to think about where Daria is now.

Apparently Daria is in Norfolk.

That is far too far away. Norwich. Can my father paint a Norwich scene, quickly. No.

By now they have reached Devizes. The signals are strong. They are entering Devizes museum. I knew all along they would come in here, where I am hanging. Next to me is another picture of myself, Alice Balancing. I face into the wall in this. Rather, my face looks into the scene, at our old pear tree; only the back of my head is visible. Past the pear tree there's a lovely shamanic flower bed composed not of plant or vegetable anything but of sparkling little red, blue and silver squares. I'm holding a big pole and balancing on this stick of wood in the grass.

I like that, says Maurice. It's very life-like.

But look at that flower bed.

I like that too.

She'll get wet. It's going to rain. See the clouds behind.

Pete, says Maurice, you can be so fanciful at times. What are you going to do about Daria?

Only the gods know, I don't. I can't live with her and I can't imagine living without her. And I still love her.

He looks at the picture: It's a balancing act, you might say.

Maurice: It's not a balancing act.

No, you're right, it's not.

Pete and Maurice turn back to the picture of me falling, where I am conducting the affairs of the world.

I almost wish someone would tell me what to do, says Pete.

Or just flip a coin.

I'm too old for that.

Anyone can flip a coin. Put yourself in the hands of the gods. You flip it.

All right. Heads.

I stare at Maurice and he stares at me. I am falling, falling. The bookcase is falling too, but it's solid. Falling free are the urn, two leaves and a five of diamonds.

Heads what?

Heads you stay.

I may be falling but I'm firm. My feet touch nowhere but my father has me squarely the right way up. He had my hair combed down my back, straight and true, not ruffled by the rush of the air. The falling doesn't trouble me, I'm strong.

Flip it again.

Heads.

All right, says Pete. I'll stay.

I move forward fifteen years. We park the car. We sit in the dark. There's a starry sky; the stars are large and close. Something calls, hoots. Suddenly a great brown owl flies across the slope of Silbury hill.

Sisters

Stand waiting to sing at the silvery microphone. The song text is taped to the stand, the backing music will come through the headphones. Check your distance. Not the yards to the gates and the road, lined by the dark cypresses, where at some time Michael will arrive. I don't mean, either, that two miles to the nearest town, pale Llucmajor, where Michael might pass through. Check simply those careful centimetres to the microphone. Look down to your feet: your spot has been marked by yellow tape on the floor. Willy himself jerked the tape from a roll, cut strips with scissors and stuck them there. (He held me by the arms showing me where to stand, held me in his blue-eyed gaze. I smelled his hair gel. He deliberately brushed my nipples; that's Willy. But I ignored this because I know I am too strong for him, he will not have me, nor my sister.)

I'm alone with Willy and Terry the dog at his studio outside pale Llucmajor, in the middle of nowhere.

The town at least is on maps. Far from tourist trails, it's a dusty *pueblo* of closed shutters in the statutory Mallorcan green. Where are we geographically? Splice Mallorca down the middle and you would go cleanly through Llucmajor's Plaça d'Espanya, on Sundays turning it to a rubble of apricots and almond shells and fine shoes; on days like today turning it to plain dust; leaving an Iberian Mediterranean to the left and Italian Med to the right. (Think Mediterranean without the water: olives, citruses, fireflies, but no blue seas thick with life; this is dry land on the Mallorcan plain.)

It is the final day for recording, set aside for putting down the last singing track and a piano solo.

My sister Chrissie will pass through that dusty square with Michael, whom we are extremely lucky to have, *excited* to have. I'm willing them to arrive, don't let them stop in Llucmajor.

"Wait for it, Denise." My eyes meet Willy's blue-eyed gaze, black and silver bristle, his glistening tan. "Before you give me soul—" I give him a quizzical look: Soul? "You know what I mean, Denise—your soul. Before you do, first I have to cut back that echo. Give me one minute. Two."

Two minutes to imagine Michael and Chrissie on the Harley-Davidson. I picture them already leaving the square, passing the statue in homage to the shoemakers of Llucmajor before building up speed. I imagine them glimpsing, laid out on trays, apricots which have been halved to look like ears; revving past the empty outskirts of the town at siesta. Soon to draw up at the studio, to buzz the intercom. It takes a minute for Willy to go to the gates with Terry, a golden Labrador, an unlikely breed to protect recording equipment in the middle of nowhere.

Terry is the same colour as the town. Terry and Willy, two lone dogs.

Our souls are very small and difficult to see and find. This is because they are not in our hearts but in a drop of blood. This drop of blood may be used once in a lifetime.

The drop of blood is encircled by barbed wire.

Listen: the technology is perfect. Listening through the headphones is like hearing outer space, hearing nothing. When I push the headphones half-off both ears: not even the air-conditioning, nothing. If Llucmajor is on maps, the studio is on nothing, amid nothing. Beyond the silvery microphone, past the sliding glass doors of the studio: *nada*. The half-dozen cypresses, rippling and waving. Indigo-grey clouds, set fast in the sky. To the right, a patio with a white table and chairs. No life the other side of the glass doors except sporadic forays by Terry, sniffing and searching the haphazard searches of a dog. Beyond him, in the driveway of cracked concrete, between kerbs of cheap brown tiles: still nothing. Panning left, there is that old Citroen stopped in the grass, between bamboo clumps; a delivery van with rusted blue and silver panels, halted for ever just short of the swimming pool, an indecipherable name above its twin windscreens. An *N*, a *G*, possibly *IR* at the end.

Still Willy is sliding the switches at the console. Captain on the bridge, he adjusts dials, swivels aside on his black leather chair. What are we waiting for? Where are Michael and Chrissie at this very moment? "Nearly there, Denise." He and Michael are so different. Yesterday Willy said: I would like a young air hostess—as if he was hungry for some juicy chicken.

"Ready. Watch the third line again," he says pushing his sunglasses firmly up in his hair. "My brother knows where the *best bars* are. Aim for *best bars* the whole time. So it's best bars."

But a phone rings: Willy disappears from his place at the console. A bridge with no captain. I re-tape the text (*Crescent City* by Lucinda Williams) to the music stand, hang the headphones on the headphone stand.

I leave the room to stroll to the Citroen. It's warm out. Years before, the van must have been driven across the neighbouring plot to stop at the pool. At its tail the rusted roof of a rusted counter is propped open still, like a roadside stall selling fish, eggs. I hear the cypresses. I walk over and touch one as cars zip by, headed west towards Palma, causing the branches to spring back and forth. Terry barks and I head back past the pool, a pit of leaves and brown stains. There goes a red dragonfly, quivering. I stroke Terry behind the ears and he beats his tail against some bamboo. Other than the Citroen, he's the only attraction. The count of activities between takes is: three strolls to the Citroen to two playing with Terry, to one encounter listening to takes and watching the seismographs of sound on the screen, fielding Willy's flirtations. I see there's a tree with blue plums beside the studio wall.

Slipping through the sliding doors I reinstall myself at the stands and the headphones and the tape on the floor and the silvery microphone.

Willy comes back brashly, ripping the wrapper off a Mars bar, a panther with a lump of meat. Energised, as if he's been vigorously showering. As if he and his hostess have been fucking. Something I don't want to think about. "OK Denise. How come you don't look really like your sister, by the way?" I don't answer; I dangle my arms. "I mean, you *are* twins, mm?" "What's that to do with you?" "Just wondering, Denise. No sweat." "Chrissie was in a bad way for a long time; ill. That's what made her so thin." "You two are so different," says Willy ignoring this information, "yesterday it crossed my mind you might have been after Michael; *interested*. Today I thought: So how come Chrissie's the one on the motorbike?" He stops chewing and scrunches the wrapper, dropping it carefully in a bin. "Denise?" "She likes motorbikes. Can't you spare me your inanities?" "Sure, I'm very short on inanities." "Well then." "We're all set. Sing into the mike from any side, any way you want. Could be the last take. Best bars."

Burly Michael is astride his Harley-Davidson with Chrissie behind clutching what she can of his great girth. Barely able to see in front of him, she drops her head to look back one last time at the valley of Sóller, the sprawl of town and sprinkling of orange plantations. She looks up and the silvery forks of the handlebars dip and twist through a narrow gorge. She leans with Michael. Under the mountains the road is clear; they roar through the cool tunnel connecting Sóller with the Mallorcan plain. Michael accelerates. Chrissie shuts her eyes, trying not to suck in tarry air. Underground video cameras would catch big Michael in sunglasses, turning to grey his French-blue aertex shirt; would see Chrissie in a sweatshirt, without the pink hoops on grey. It seems they are below the mountains only a matter of instants, before Chrissie, eyes still shut, feels her eyelids turn orange, filtering light. Out of the tunnel, back in the sun—still ten miles from pale Llucmajor—and groves of olive and almond trees fly by, attached to pale *fincas* set back from the road. Chrissie feels magnetised by a sense of adventure.

For a few hundred yards they draw alongside the rattling carriages of the old Sóller train. Michael glances at it; a boy waves; the boy would see Michael's greying hair beneath his helmet, Chrissie's blondness fluttering. The Harley veers back to the centre line. They bear down on a station; the road arcs away from the tracks. Chrissie inhales lungfuls of happiness. She looks at her watch: they are making excellent time. They speed on, over the plain of La Pla towards the mountains of Randa and Llucmajor, where Michael is to lay down his piano solo.

People say Michael is a musical genius.

I said to Chrissie: Chrissie, I hope for poetry. I pray.

After that: I pray he will want me.

Willy's studio may be in the middle of nowhere but access to it is dangerous. The blue gates with their spikes and alarms (for show, admits Willy) shut directly onto the road. As a car waits at the intercom, its rear blocks the road and a sudden chicane forms on the C171, the fast straight crossing the dry fields between Palma and pale Llucmajor. Those Spanish cars fly past at eighty, ninety miles an hour. A crazy car could crash into you as you wait. Does Willy care? Willy? Willy cares about Willy. He has Terry and he has glacier-blue eyes and an expensive studio and no other cares; he has no wife or air hostess in the back or anywhere.

Nonetheless he is worth having for his work, his energy. Willy is energy, Chrissie reckons. Sometimes misdirected. But energy is good, good for making music. Energy is good for lovemaking, but not always enough. Chrissie says he would not be tender with a woman.

Would Michael be tender?

I can see my sister leaning, catching sight of him, unable to make out his words, and him leaning back, guessing at hers. The Harley decelerates majestically to turn off the main highway, for Bunyola.

She presses a hand on Michael's great shoulder. I want to stop, she shouts in his ear.

Here?

I've been loving it so much, she says as the revs die. I want to feel there's a second ride to come.

The Harley pop-pops to a halt by a field. They lift off their helmets. Michael's shoulders are brown against the blue of his shirt. Chrissie walks about, stretching and shaking her legs. Michael sits against a grey stone wall, his hands behind his head.

Chrissie, he says, you and I can go for a ride any time.

My sister—Denise is wondering if you're going straight back home. After the recordings are done.

No, I don't think so.

She'll be pleased. We'll all be pleased.

Ah, don't tell me, Chrissie, you are trying to precipitate events—

We are sisters.

I like Denise, of course.

God what are *those*?

Those are watermelons.

On the *ground*? Like *that*? I thought they always had stripes.

We can take one with us. Or look for a striped one in Llucmajor. They'll have all kinds.

Let's not stop there.

We should. It's a historical town.

Chrissie reaches over and strokes him on the chin, her hand barely touching. Or does she? Would she do this?

Historical? she says. As in what?

This would be a familiar talk, I heard it from him last night as we ate fish from the grill and drank wine. Chrissie had turned in, leaving us alone at the big hotel table under the vines and the fairy lights. It was warm out still.

Does history matter? Michael can make you think it does.

It was just our second encounter.

He sat across from me. There were dishes and bottles and paper and pieces of bread strewn about the table.

I recognised you by the beach this afternoon, I said. You were deep in a book.

Yes, he said. Getting my bearings in Mallorca.

I'm reading *A Winter in Mallorca* by George Sand.

Well, he said, two people reading. It's an ancient art.

Reading is?

Yes, he said: reading is.

I sipped my wine. There were stars out over the mountains. Reading is. I asked about his book. It was a history book.

Long ago, under the same stars, there were kings of Mallorca. The last, Jaume III, was killed in battle at Llucmajor. He had striven to reclaim the island from his hated cousin of Aragón, who had held it for six years. By the time they were reinstalled on the island, Jaume's forces were sick, debilitated, and they fought. Jaume was beheaded by a common soldier. It was 1349.

Michael looked at me steadily as he poured himself water.

I've looked carefully at the map, he said.

What map? I asked.

Several maps.

You like to be thorough.

I am.

Is it also an ancient art?

Being thorough? I don't know.

Apparently, careful study of these maps revealed the very path of C171 was the line of march taken by Jaume's army. On this ancient track, Jaume passed Willy's studio going east, that is, from left to right. The following week the armies of Aragón tramped by in the same direction. Another week and the same armies of Aragón, but reduced slightly in volume, passed back from right to left. There followed a week empty of marching armies. Willy and Terry would have waited, looking right, listening for the sound of feet from the right, in a march that never came. Jaume's army did not, could not, would not pass again. In the week following that week of waiting, Mallorca was declared definitively part of Spain.

"Denise I was just aiming to be friendly."

"Back, Willy. Just put the coffee in the cup. Then push it this way."

"Why sit so far off? I don't bite, Denise. Come on."

"It's a big table out here. I'll sit where I like."

It's no use telling Willy about souls, but the drop of blood of a singer may appear in one word on one note in one song. Everyone has their drop, which may appear in a remark, a gesture, an insight. A kiss.

Even then, only the persons themselves may be aware they are showing their souls. Recognising them is almost impossible.

"Something to eat, Denise?"

"No thanks. Why do you keep calling me Denise?"

"Isn't it obvious. Or would you prefer something more—more tender?"

"No. Let's change the subject."

Does Willy have a soul? Surely, somewhere, even Willy. This place has a soul: in an old rusting van. A line of dark trees.

"OK Denise. Change to what? Do you *know* any air hostesses? Flight attendants?"

"Forget it, Willy. Do you think we'll make money on all this?"

"We have to. Or we have a problem. And we have a problem anyway."

"What?"

"Because, Denise, as I don't need to tell you—our young customers out there don't buy their music any more. What's more, they don't even have to *decide* what to buy, because they don't buy. They don't need to discern what's good and what isn't. And it's good to be able to choose, it makes you—"

"—stronger"

"Stronger, thank you. Denise. Now I'm a discerning person."

"I was wondering about that."

"I choose you."

"I choose Michael."

"Well, that's illuminating."

"It's been an illuminating break, Willy. For you at least."

"It'll be the last. It's back to work. I make it *tres horas*."

I see the Plaça waiting for them like a film set. Its narrow triangle, dull as dust. The church dominates less like a church in a square than a silo in a field. There are shut doors, a dingy supermarket, the red-awninged Bar Tabú and white Café Colón. Will they stop there, and where will they go? Willy and I ate breakfast to a jangle of discotheque music in the Bar Tabú. Café Colón—we saw through the doors—has marble-topped tables and white crockery painted brown and swirlingly Café Colón, but is even more dead to business than the bar.

The Harley draws up, or does it draw up? If it draws up, it will be not to local consternation but to indifference. Indifference, because there is something impenetrable about Llucmajor: impenetrability is a crimson thread running through it. It is crunchy nuts and handmade shoes, is old discotheque music and marble together. Llucmajor is as exciting as a tablecloth; such is its soul.

(For the soul of a place, unlike that of a person, is never disguised; is precisely what is on view; is as it appears.)

My talk with Willy has cut a knot. Now I can sing fulsomely. I can see Michael in front of me and I can't describe the moment we kiss but I think there must be many opportunities for people who want this, if he wants this, and I sense he is coming to want it.

"That's it, Denise. Just drop everything, leave it where it is."
"Finished?"
"Just Mike now."
Damn right, Willy. I leave the silvery microphone, go and join him and Terry in the next room. He's in the thrall of his switches. Now I'm done I'm less tense. I feel like I've been drinking wine. Last night we drank enough. I can still see Michael pushing back the table to make more room for himself.

So what, he asked, befell George Sand?

I was able to tell him that after a dire winter on Mallorca with a sick Chopin, she claimed Mallorcans were a lazy bunch, lazy for not exploiting the natural riches of their island. Instead of turning more pesos by, say, organising the transportation of more oranges to a second port as well as a first, they mooched off and ate the oranges themselves. They sat around playing cards.

Also an art, said Michael.

We looked at each other without wavering.

Reading is.

Thoroughness may be.

I remember too thinking: to George Sand Mallorca lived in an air of defeat. It felt like a dilute version of what it could have been.

She could have claimed that King Jaume's contribution, his drop of blood, had been to leave the island with this desultory air. So ignoble are souls sometimes.

If we lie in bed together I will tell him about souls. When we lie there.

Forget the stripes on the melons. Let's skip Llucmajor, Michael. We can reach Willy's down the back roads.

OK Chrissie. That may be shorter.

We go so fast.

Do you want us to go slower?

No. It's a thrill.

I had plucked a plum from the tree beside the studio and was peering in through the windscreens of the Citroen, wondering if animals might use a rusted old van, and what animals could these be, when I heard a motorbike stop at the gates and heard the buzzer press for Willy and heard Terry bark and heard desperate tyres. The plum was full of juice. I felt the juice on my chin just before I heard the motorbike approaching, I guessed it was them. The juice felt good, in the way I had come to realise that all excess, trying everything, can feel so good. I had put everything into those songs, as I knew Michael would too. The moment I heard the Harley I ran with Terry to greet him.

Freewheeling

Wearying, bored after the revelries in the *Quartier Latin*, or, who knows, simply to evade the cool of the morning, a mosquito slips through an open window. Drawn by the warmth yet discomforted by dry pools of air, it explores the rooms, noting Emmy and me with our mattress in the living room, under a sheet on our sides, kissing hard. Sidestepping the exotic towering plant with its leaves streaming down in ribbons, it whines about our ageing heads and Emmy flaps at an ear. Satisfied at the situation and, who knows again, thinking it wiser to wait until we grow still, this mosquito the size of an eyelash retires to the kitchen to relax, tap the blinding sun, yellow as lemon, streaming along the rue Clovis across la place Sainte Geneviève, past the Panthéon and onto the kitchen table—where it alights at the edge of a shadow. *Listen.* No wings beat. The fridge whirs. Wary of the glare from bright papers, its monitoring instinct for carbon dioxide and humidity continuing like a heartbeat, it double-checks the apartment from front to back, mapping the radiators, the places with water and the corners for retreating to. There it goes, out of reach of a sudden snort of pleasure
people are strange
reach of our gentle moans, the open window, the electrostatic heat from the music system, before returning in security to

the table, to almost precisely the same place, the same shadow which has shifted with the sun. *Stay unpredictable*. The situation is good. No competing female within radius, no distracting males. Instantly it moves to an area of white wall above the table. *Don't move*. A ticking sound. Moans.

strange: pain and pleasure sound the same

The fridge rattles to a stop. Still no wings beat. No water runs; no human tread lumbers. Lightheaded now, the mosquito skips about a scattering of crumbs. Again quickly bored, or to kill time, it peruses the sports columns of *Le Monde*, tries a puzzle and gives up, works out from the correspondence on the table that Emmy and I are alone in the apartment (on loan from the absent Simone), and when twenty minutes have passed on the microwave clock and our moans still not ceased it goes straight to where Emmy is brushing the delightfully cusped soles of her feet against me—the rocking, the clasping arms, Jesus, Emmy, my knuckled hand gripping at the mattress.

It bites.

perfect

We slow down, pause, stop altogether. Winter's on the way for God's sake, curses Emmy at the whine, now disappeared. *Goddamn!* she says in the delectable Texan *twayung* she has most when she's fired up (Anytime I git talkin' that way it's becuz I'm feelin' so *good*, honey—not that she was feeling good just then). *Who woulda thunk it?* I wait for her to say, but she doesn't. Standing with her tall self bent over, she scratches furiously at that expensively-cut short white hair with both hands; not a flake of skin or dust floats down.

God*damn*, she says. If anythin' can git me hyperventilatin' it is all this fixin' to git here alone, the trains and cheques and the stories we been tellin' at home, I even got a court in Houston holdin' on fer a week jus' fer me, and a damn *bug* thinks nothing of extendin' his stay into November. These guys think they can jus' come an' go as they please.

I turn my head slowly, scouring the air and for harmony's sake deciding not to point out marauding mosquitoes must be female.

Above me, over the mantelpiece and reappearing by the morning light, the great head of the green and black cow signed Uriburu 1975 looks steadily past us down the length of the living room. As ever it is blind to whatever moves, be it Emmy's swagger as she walks off to the bathroom, the curtain-like leaves from the towering plant rustling and settling after her passing, or me waving a hand in front of its big cow eyes, or scratching at the knuckle of a finger, getting up to have Bob Dylan deliver Thunder on the Mountain on the CD player. Uriburu: it is a good thirty years since this cow took over the foreground to an industrial dairy looking like a Guggenheim museum, smoke pluming back for miles, turned its enormous head with its great ears, nostrils gleaming with mucus, and froze there. Since then its interest has been confined to the far side of rooms. For years now the Uriburu cow has been contemplating the picture opposite, a sight like stones at dusk, quiet grey and black and blue pastel with patches of ochre: artwork by Estève, dated 1968, where the mosquito has settled.

Emmy returns looking clean and scrubbed, flushed.

Shower's free, honey. Brr, it's cold when you jus' got outta the bathroom.

She yanks the tie to her shiny grey dressing gown. I stretch, pretending I'm still young. I show my fingers.

Is that what it did to yuh? she says kneeling. Aw, yuh been bit. You impressed?

Some. But I seen some sights already. Git a spring chicken if you want to make yuhself an impression. But neither of us should worry none, when I find it I'll *kill* it. It's on these walls someplace. Y'hear? Yew gonna stand lookin' at that ol' cow all day? Jus' what has that cow got that I ain't?

There's history on these walls. This is Simone's mother as a child.

Emmy rolls her shoulders inside her grey gown and looks at this drawing on the mantelpiece, a picture I'd known down all the years I'd known Simone. The little girl on a chaise-longue looking at a big flat book. A figure with a critical, I am my own person expression, dress short, long socks, legs crossed, hard-heeled shoes with simple buckles; scrawled above: *hommage respectueux*, Brest, 30.12 1925.

She's like your English Alice. And who's this?

A little photo of Simone herself is tucked inside the frame. This her? Emmy says; I nod.

See her hand? Emmy says. See how her fingers go dippin'? Maybe she's been bitten.

If she'd been bit she wouldn't be smilin'.

Damn Texan lawyers, I'm thinking. I put my arm round her waist. Dippedy d—

zipa zee ay ay
beautiful wings
keep still now

Yew jus' stop that, darlin'. And don't you start callin' me Tammy or Patsy-Jo an' askin' for grits and *frahd pahs* or any of that.

Or, I said enjoying myself: talking about the *awl* business.

Yew think you are hotter than a two-dollar pistol, but go on this way an' we are gonna be makin' other arrangements, or rather I'm gonna be, you hear? Yew jus' look. She looks to me like she's rappin', she's a child rapper ahead of her time.

She's a pixie, I say, a six-year-old pixie in around 1950.

Sure.

Emmy and I look at each other straight on. Our eyes are dull with age, their browns cloudy where they once shone. But her lips make a bow like on a present.

Peace?

Peace. I fergotten what is was we got to be arguin' about.

We kiss hard. Her face is close, she's looking down at my lips. I'm goin' to get you tonight, honey. Gonna getcha.

We breakfasted on an enormous *chausson normand* pastry, sugary with pieces of apple. Christine, I said referring to my wife, would be horrified. At this sweet *stuff*, I mean.

Day-un too, said Emmy, not that I know when that may-uhn was las' horrified at any ol' thing. But don't you go thinkin' about that, she said stroking my cheek. You an' me are seein' the sweet side of life.

Assumin' as I am, she adds between kisses, that you will be lookin' your best as we get outta here. I don't wunt us goin' someplace and you arrivin' like a flower.

low, low vibrations
Estève is perfect
Estève is mosquito art
So, as
we straightened the sheets and made lists and Emmy became engrossed at the next picture along

I swear all these pictures roun' here are like mirrors, the way they all look out at yew. D'ya git whut I mean? Like they are tryin' to tell us somethin'. But what?

I don't know.

An' there's all these gener*ations*. Ev'ry twenty-five years there's a picture. Yew noticed that?

Like a cycle?

Somethin' like that. Our lives are such a mystery, I reckon. If yew ever stop and reckon.

rates with a Jackson Pollock
as we left the apartment and strolled in the Luxembourg gardens, astonished at the tobacco plants flowering (November, for God's sake), struck by raspberry and red stockings, hearing Arabic, the chess player in a witch's hat, the children's sailing boats with their filthy red-white-and-blue sails

as we decided to visit the Père Lachaise cemetery:
the mosquito, engorged, stayed put and slept, eggs maturing thinking knuckles and ankles and forearms.

As we took the Métro and at the cemetery entrance had our next argument, over buying a decent guide (Emmy in the pro camp, thorough as always) although I had a thumbnail map in my guidebook, but Emmy was tough, *crusty* she calls it, as tough as perhaps they all are in Texas, and I relented, after all neither of us wanted to miss Jim Morrison and Emmy threatened separation and retraction of all promises if we did not see the tombs of Edith Piaf and Oscar Wilde.

As under a clear sky we walked the cobbled chunky-kerbed streets, rising and dipping and bending.

As Emmy oohed and ahhed and sighed her way through her guide. Apparently we stood where the first creatures of note in Paris had lived: elephant-like mammoths had tumbled down this very hillside to drink at the Seine.

Balzac had a polished black slab and fresh flowers, Colette had similar in pink. Oscar Wilde had graffiti; Edith Piaf great pale peonies. We observed the fashion for visitors to take photographs beside their celebrities, the fashion for dark blue roses whose significance we were not aware of; but the one long blue rose that lay at a slant on the grave of Jim Morrison of the Doors, hemmed in by other graves, seemed appropriate. By his grave a scowling young man held off to one side, waiting and waiting for the groups to disperse: the pale-skinned mademoiselles, blue-haired, orange-haired, the couples, singles, drugged out, necrophiliacs, bus parties, pensioners, practisers of dark sex, sorcery, who knows. Emmy quoted from her book. Louis XV: I should like to be loved. Jim Morrison: I am loved. But, Emmy said, buht. He had such a dark side, I don't understan' it. Now if Bobby Dylan were buried jus' here instead, I would kinda prefer it. Didya ever see that picture of him on the cover with that girl walkin' down the street in the snow.

Freewheeling, I said. What a good pic*shur*.

Yew stop that yuh hear. Yew think you are the brightest crayon in the box, but jus' maybe yew ain't.

motionless

As: I told Emmy she could light my fire but she said I would not be lighting anything of hers in the near future. Don't you love her madly? Love me two times. I stopped this when we came to the wall where 147 members of the 1871 Paris Commune had been chased across the cemetery, hopping about the tombstones like rabbits, my guide said—marched through, said hers—and shot up against that very wall. Nearby, victims of the holocaust were remembered. Here everyone slowed, and clouds from nowhere turned the day dark, and in this new dark day crows moved in and perched on sepulchry. The sky blackened; the groups hastened to the exits; in the distance, where Jim Morrison lay, the young man stepped up to claim the space beside his grave.

As we were going back quietly; taking in Paris. We went via the *fnac* store to buy songs by the Doors. Finally we passed through the big doors to the apartment-cum-library building, to the little Otis lift, mosquito-less—*Charge Maximum 300 kg 4 Personnes*. While clanking to our floor, the DÉPARTEMENT DES AFFAIRES GÉNÉRALES, we pressed against each other. No honey, no, Emmy said. The only thing I'm ridin' raht now is the elevator, now who would have thunk it, there's our stop.

Were we having an *affaire générale*? I asked Emmy with the key in the door.

Yew are so dumb. An' ugly as a mud fence.

But I'm in the *awl bidness*.

Yew are not, she said pushing me away. And don't yew go gettin' me worked up like that.

She slapped my backside. Yew ol' cowpoke.

I'm a cowpoke?

Yew certainly are. All hat and no cattle.

Across the roofs the Eiffel tower was lit up again. The lights came on for ten minutes on the hour. Like a sparkler, said Emmy, though my guidebook said it looked like champagne.

I put on the Doors.

that's something I can vibrate to

As: we passed within feet of the picture like stones at dusk, quiet grey and black and blue pastels with patches of ochre—I thought

restless

I thought I saw a stone shift—to wash and change before going out to eat at the Polidor in rue Monsieur le Prince, where it was claimed Ho Chi Minh had washed up.

The place was packed. We rehashed thoughts about the mosquito.

Saying Ho Chi Minh was back there in that room washing up, I said small-talking a way through the din of excited voices, the clatter of plates and carafes and glasses: is like saying I've got A positive blood. How can you prove it?

Have yew?

Got A positive blood? Actually no.

Well then you haven't. Yew have already contradicted yewself an' yew ain't been in the stand a half minute.

You're so smart, Emmy.

So everyone tells me, an' they cain't all be wrong. Whereas I am A positive.

You are?

I'm tellin' yew.

You can't prove it.

Why should I prove it? I know it.

Zeut! Our neighbour at the long table was poking at pink spots in the liver on his plate. Was a mosquito choosy? We focused on the menu. Emmy ate fish and I had guinea fowl. We ate *bavarois cassis* together. Its dark syrup around a soft square of pink made a thick pool on the white plate.

Like bluh-uhd, I said to goad Emmy.

Yew know what we say when somethin' tastes this good? It's larrupin'.

Larrupin.

There you go, yew learn somethin' everyday and yew are goin' be all right.

All *raht*, you mean.

Yew ol' cuss, yew are goin' to git it. Yew will be the cute little English boy no more. I'm fixin' to cut it off in the night and jus' throw it them.

As: we missed the glittering on the Eiffel Tower on the hour, but the shopfronts lit the streets. At a square on the rue Mouffetard where some fig trees still thrived, we had hot drinks to finish the day.

We were back out of the clanking lift to catch the lights at eleven. We had music on low.

As Emmy walked back from the bathroom and took off her gown.

people are strange

I put my clothes on a chair. I looked at her in the dim light of the one lamp left on.

I jus' didn't think this would happen agin, she said unclipping her earrings.

No?

Try more than no.

Yes.

Yew are dumber than dirt. How about some romance? Jus' a little?

Is that what you mean by 'this'?

An' this, she underlined, reaching under the sheet. Have I got to slow down everythin' jus' so yuh can keep up? Didya know Jim Morrison and myself are one and the same age?

Him again.

He bother you some? He was better than yew, I guess.

Just a minute there.

Same age as him, give or take a week, I fergit which.

Doesn't show.

How would it ever show? He is forever young. The same age, and I still like sex.

Em—

I like it, she said poking my chest, a whole lot.

I was stuck for replies.

It went for the next knuckle along.

satisfactory

heavier now

slower

The itching woke me. I got up.

I looked across at the student library in the night. Empty of studiers, but the watery green reading lights were still burning. As if something important had to be kept going. What was this thing? The boards creaked as I walked back to Emmy. Past dark Estève, past wide-eyed Uriburu. Emmy in her sleep still as anything, pale against the blue pillows. Who could guess anything about Emmy from seeing her this way? An hour's legal consultancy with Emmy costs the earth; but who would have thunk it. The sparkle ran up and down the Eiffel Tower again; its beacon lights swept round. Emmy twitched in her sleep.

Next it was morning.

My ankles, Emmy was saying. *Goddamn!* Look. And look there.

She had Tiger Balm. We smeared it on my knuckles and her ankles.

We became a search party after the common enemy. Emmy kept insisting it was male—that guy is *bay*-uhd.

Em, you're the icing on their cake.

I thought I was on your cake, said Emmy in an invisible cloud of camphorous Tiger Balm. So am I to take it I am *none* of those things you been sayin'?

Our plan was to visit the Jeu de Paume, newly reopened. Instead the search cut into our day as we inspected every wall, down to the skirting boards, under the radiators.

We went out to buy newspapers and magazines. Empty boxes marked CHAMPAGNE were stacked in the streets. In the daytime the Eiffel Tower was dull brown and dry. Three days left to us and we lazed, reading about film stars and headscarves and the New Orleans floods. Near the Rhode Island-Massachusetts border, an article said, an outbreak of disease spread by mosquitoes had terrified entire towns.

After our ritual gazing at the sparkling champagne running up and down the tower we called our partners and told them what we had been up to, I with my old friend Simone in the rue Mouffetard and the cemetery at Père Lachaise (she took a photo of me there with Jim Morrison), Emmy with her old friend Simone in the rue Mouffetard and the cemetery at Père Lachaise (she took a photo of me there with Jim Morrison). Don't let anybody judge us, Emmy said sharply: life is too short. Her countryman Bob Dylan had us both singing *I got the porkchops, she got the pie / She ain't no angel and neither am I*. When yew were young, I mean, younger, said Emmy lying there, did—

iiiiiiiii

I smacked my head and felt dizzy.

Oh boy. You've got to see it first, Emmy said. No good jus' havin' conniptions.

iiiiiieeeeee

Put your arm out for bait, I told Emmy.

Pert out your own arm fer bay-uht.

I'd have to be crazy.

It whined by our ears then I saw it, clapped ⇘ my hands.

Damn it, I told Emmy as I looked at two empty hands, you've got to be quick.

Yew are jus' one expert, she said hugging me. Ugh, my *God!*

My hands weren't empty. A mark stained the base of one thumb. I smeared it quickly; blood spread on my palm.

That's your blu-uhd, honey, said Emmy.

Looks like A positive to me.

Darlin', yew are mis*take*n. No way that is ever A *any*thin'. You happy?

I guess so. I jus' didn' like sayin' it.

I'm listening.

Since yew and I are talkin' like we are and messin' like we are—

And freewheeling.

And freewheelin' an' all I may as well tell yuh. If I felt any better I might jus' drop my harp clean through the cloud.

How Technology Can Burn Down Your Home

Only God and the fiction writer can present an account of the cause of the fire which burned the house down. Certainly the Fortunes, Annabel and Dan, were in no position to explain it. The fire was long out, cold, the remains black and moistened by rain, the banister post taking a new, valiant pride of place, by the time they returned from their fortnight in Perpignan. In the sequel to the fire—their arrival by taxi to discover their home gone, flowerbeds smouldering, fridge slumped against the drum which faithfully used to wash their clothes; a row of books in a long charcoal curve on the ground, strange wires which had once been housed in Annabel Fortune's piano lid glued sadly to a last blackened wall—indeed a scene begging for the fiction writer to move over for the filmmaker—they paid the taxi driver in slow, languid motion, their jaws locked in disbelief, mouths refusing to close until strange smells hit them, as they stood with their suitcases and cardboard tubes of Salvador Dali posters before the charred site of the house in High Barnet they claimed to have cherished and loved.

Leaping across from the sink, the cat gathered its entire weight on the touch-sensor controls of the cooker and, jumping at an answering electro-computerised squeak, catching sight of shadows not knowing they were its own reflections in the ceramic top, shunted the setting of a hot plate onto 9 and started other hot plates on and off and back again, *youch*, until the reddening rings interrupted its pouncings to send it yowling behind the piano (as it was then) in the living room.

Far away, on the wrong side of the Channel and the Massif Central, Annabel and Dan Fortune were just three days into their holiday.

But wait. Only God and the fiction writer, and possibly Sherlock Holmes, can explain how a cat could be left to itself in a house, so alone and unsupervised. Over to Sherlock, the transcendent detective. May his aura descend on the charred remains. There are tins of food for cats but no remains of a cat, Watson. No bones. And see that blackened frame under this tarpaulin, this is the kitchen door that was. How do you know? It has a lock, see, and it lies at the back of the plot. I see, but what about it? It has no cat flap. No cat flap, Holmes, well, not much use for one now, is there, if you get my drift? Watson, you can be most humourful but this will not serve the purpose of true detective work. We shall make enquiries of the neighbours next door. To do this we shall first scale this garden wall at the back of their house. We will, Holmes? Very well, I will. Then I shall meet you round the front, hurry Watson. Holmes, why so fast, I'll be there right away! Ding dong. Mrs Flowers? Sherlock Holmes. Not *the* Sherlock Holmes?

Indeed, Mrs Flowers, he is. You are Dr Watson? I am, I am *the* Dr Watson, may we come in? Sit here Mr Holmes, excuse my atrocious cold. I thank you Mrs Flowers, we shall not detain you long. I am guessing you were detailed to look after the cat, but, if I am not mistaken, something went awry in this arrangement. Funny you should say that, Mr Holmes, *the* Mr Holmes—but I can't believe it, you must have been alive at least a hundred and fifty years to be able to speak to me now. That's all right, Mrs Flowers. It's all right, what's all right about it? I'm a device, you might say Mrs Flowers. A *device*? Let's say: I've been commissioned to take on this case by the insurers, partners in

Kentish Town. But to return to the cat. Ah, the cat, well on the day of the night of the fire, I *saw* the cat in my garden. It was definitely her, down to the red collar. She must have got out somehow: probably through a tiny window on the top floor, I deduced from my knowledge of the property. But I knew she could never get back the same way. No more than I could jump out of my own bedroom window and expect to be able to cata-pult back to bed from down on the ground. So I went straight in the house and closed the window. Then straight out again? And you smelled nothing suspicious on account of your cold? That's right, Mr Holmes, how did you know?

Certainly you were not in there long enough to notice the fire. Indeed it can hardly have begun. What time were you there? About seven. Then the fire began at seven, seven-fifteen. Holmes, you're brilliant. But what about the cat, Mrs Flowers, what did you do about the cat? Oh, I put out some crunchy Friskies and cream and next thing I know she was staying with me. Nowadays they say cats don't actually like cream but this one does. Here's Cindy now. See the collar. Between you and me, they could have called her *Cinders*. Cinders, I see Mrs Flowers, Cinders. I'm in poor taste of course Mr Holmes, but poor taste can be interesting. If you don't agree, if I'm just too much for you, perhaps you'd rather talk to my husband—known variously as Alan and Mr F. Heavens no, Mrs Flowers, we are delighted to be speaking to you. You're so kind, Dr Watson. Speak no further, dear lady, it is apparent to all that you are kindness itself. Holmes?

One last question: when did you raise the alarm? Ah: I was fearful you would put this to me. Fearful? Because I didn't. Round here we *rely* on one another, so I suppose everyone thought—do you know, I don't think anyone raised an alarm. Mr F said it was probably blazing all evening until a fire engine just happened to trundle by on its way to the station. Which we didn't see either, come to think of it. And of course once the fire was out there was no fire to report. Oh dear, Mrs Flowers, I see and I don't see. Yes, Dr Watson. This is most embarrassing for you Mrs Flowers. especially as you would have often been in the house yourself, having been detailed to look after Cinders,

I mean Cindy. Me *and* Mr F were supposed to—are you sure you don't want to interrogate him too, he was here throughout. Arsenal were playing Real Madrid. Scaling the heights, I remember him saying. Here he is coming in the front door now, ALAN BRING IN SOME CHOCOLATE DIGESTIVES AND SEE IF WE'VE GOT ANY REAL TEA, he'll be so pleased to meet you Mr Holmes, I believe he even followed your cases when he was a young man. Mr Holmes, how do you do. Indeed I did follow them, I have a book of them on the shelf there. Somewhere in the house, anyway. But there's nothing I can tell you, I was watching the match at the time, the first half an hour was a shambles. Watching the match? said Watson, so you weren't here?—But excuse me interrupting myself, mm, these are good Mrs Flowers, did you bake these? Course I did, Dr Watson. No I didn't: McVities, I was pulling your leg. And my husband was here watching, I can vouch for him. He may be a devotee of the Premier League but he wouldn't go all the way to Madrid just for that, would you Alan? Seeing as the match was in north London Alice, no. Hm, I see, Mr Flowers, *football*, you say, shall I write that down Holmes? No Watson, just listen to Mr Flowers. Right, stop a minute Mr Holmes: what I would like to ask, now Alice don't interrupt me, to ask is: Just before you take on a case there's always some snow, or at least rain, and then there are always footprints in the flowerbeds. Not always, Mr Flowers. Or torn bits of paper with clues on them, things everyone else has astoundingly missed. Come on Holmes, enough of this. No Watson, it's all right. In this case, Mr Flowers, there were no scraps of paper, there was no snow, and although it did rain, there were no footprints, or *paw marks* even. You don't mean? said Mrs Flowers. Just Mr Holmes' little joke, Mrs Flowers, as you were saying, the name is Cindy, not Cinders, is it not. Yes, Dr Watson, I would be glad to withdraw my moment of poor taste if you'll allow me. Of course, Mrs Flowers. Mr Flowers, goodbye, and enjoy tonight's game. I hope it's not too far to travel. Goodbye, Mr Holmes, Dr Watson, and on behalf of Cinders, goodbye. *Alice*. It's just a bit of *fun*, Alan. I like to get a bit of fun out of having *Cindy*. Of course I've got to give her back to the Fortunes. Once they're back from wherever they are, and have a home again. You don't think they're *dead* do you, Mr Holmes?

In the light of this sublime detective work, that company with the household name (so argued the insurers) should never have developed its Coolcoox 56300 range of cookers with Vitramatic touch sensor controls and has a lot to answer for. God on his (/her) ownsome will deal with the company on his day of judgement (the late afternoon session; what a long day that'll be). In the division of tasks, the fiction writer is left to tidy up the awkward detail that Sherlock Holmes cannot be one hundred and fifty years old, but then he isn't, as he was not even alive a hundred and fifty years ago, having never been alive. The bald fact is that the above conversation did not take place, but was conjectured by the insurers, who liked to employ cheap methods to save money. They had thus painstakingly worked their way through every conceivable scenario (with Sherlock their device, everybody's device) in order to discover what happened while the Fortunes were at the beach, the market, on the main square in Perpignan. At seven o'clock that very evening Annabel Fortune even had a premonition.

Pernod is so powerful, Dan, it could put out fires. When it is put on flames its vapours could disperse and settle on the surrounding flames. Quashing them.
So why don't you see Red Adair drinking it?
Who's that?
Who? Only the world's most famous fire fighter. Or why don't they use it in fire extinguishers? Assuming it's compatible with the foaming mechanisms. (Dan, by the way: brown Friar Tuck hair, a dark horse emotionally speaking, bathroom-dweller. In sandals and brown shorts.)
Maybe they do, Dan. Have you ever been around when an extinguisher is on? I've only ever *seen* extinguishers, on TV. Even they probably aren't real. Not really real. (Annabel petite, tidy, also bathroom-dweller. Likewise in sandals and shorts, yellow red and green stripes.)

That's just it, Anni. Fires are things that happen to other people.

Dan, uh.

What? What?

I just had a flash that our house was on fire.

It'll be all right.

God, as long as Cindy is all right.

As long as Cindy is all right! If there was a fire my French film videos would melt to molasses.

Cindy is more important than a hundred old videos.

I don't know. There are some, many that I'd say are worth a hundred Cindys.

You can't have a hundred Cindys.

Not yet you can't. But you can have two Dollys. As in sheep. Ah, Cindy'll be all right. Mrs F will be round.

Dan, did you shut the bathroom window?

I think so. Why?

I can just see Cindy wriggling through it.

Cats don't wriggle.

They do. Where were we?

Extinguishing fires. So if you were to cough now, Anni, will your Pernod put out all the cigarettes within a twenty yard radius of here?

Twenty metres you mean.

That's even further.

I expect it would.

So much of it has been drunk around here you can't even light a match any more.

Don't say that Dan, I just get a picture of our house woofing up in flames.

OK. Let's woof it up ourselves. This is our holiday. No one even knows we're here.

That was a good idea, wasn't it, Dan?

The best.

No calls, no worries.

The Med down the road.

Already shouldering almost the entire exposition, the fiction writer must tackle another necessary question: the tangled matter of the insurance claim.

Acting on principle the Fortunes, Annabel and Dan, had resolved not to support big business and had insured their house with the small, two-woman firm who sent in Sherlock to investigate. The insurers were driven to their conjectures by the manufacturers of the cooker, which is where the electrical short circuit indisputedly occurred. These makers with the household name swore off all liability, claiming their wares were entirely safe as long as Anni or Dan had pressed the touchpad indicated by a picture of a key, a safety key, touching which rendered the cooker inoperable. Not even a cat stepping on our cooker could then turn it on, they e-mailed across London (by way of what they thought was mere illustration). Photographs were made of the Coolcoox 56300's ravaged, fire-twisted top, which looked like any hot plate left in a steel furnace overnight would look like. With the safety key unpressed, the manufacturers argued, the company could not be blamed. So: first Anni insisted she had pressed the safety switch, only to discover too late Dan had insisted he had. Too bad, the insurers mused, there were no fingerprints. Sherlock Holmes' hypothesis, despite Watson's gasping admiration, was a good bit short on actual proof, they further mused, wondering how they could still get a few K out of the makers of the cooker. But they couldn't see how. Backed by their own reinsurance, they would have to pay. In the end.

Thank God, said Annabel, thank *God* Cindy got out in time.

It's a miracle, said Mrs Flowers, she must have had feline *déjà vu*, have known something was afoot. Look at her. She is such a darling. Though you can't *cuddle* her. She's a cat.

Yes, Annabel sighed. She will sit on your lap for a minute if you're lucky.

Half a minute if you're luckier, said Dan. A quarter—

Yes, sighed Mrs Flowers, infected by her ex-neighbour's sigh. Will you ever go on holiday again?

Of course. But first we have to buy a house.

I suppose so. Though that doesn't actually follow.

What?

Ho ho, just my little moment of humour.

I can't laugh, Alice. Dan and I are only just getting over the process of denial, denying it's gone.

Well it was awful. I'd never seen a real house burned down to the ground. What a transformation. And the stench. Digestive biscuit, Dan?

Thanks Mrs F, but we've lost our appetites.

You must have! These biscuits are timeless, I was saying to Alan the other evening, *timeless*, Dan.

I wouldn't go that far, Mrs F. You do realise that recently Nabisco, who own McVities Digestives, have made a deal with Philip Morris, who own Jacob's Digestives. So the recipes may also be subject to merging, the monopolies commission. There'll be an EU Biscuits Directive.

Dan hates takeovers, Alice.

So do I, so do I. Anyway, I don't know about all this den*ying*. Don't let it beat you. If *I* was you I would try what I did when Alan and I were young. Say to yourselves: it's a *test*.

Test of what, Mrs F? Dan chipped back in.

Of your love. You and Anni.

Me and Annabel?

The two of you versus the joint strain. I confess Mr F and I don't say this any more. We did, before—

Before what?

Well, seeing as he isn't here listening. Before, before I locked the box.

What box?

You know, sex. The box of sex. I locked the box and threw away the box. Whoops, you thought I was going to say "key". But I often go for the unexpected. It's what drew Mr F to me in the first place. That and my untold millions. What a romance that was. When I first saw Mr F he was on a *bicycle*. He used to go so *evenly* on it, it's hard to communicate how much pleasure that gave me. Anyway, the key is him. So I've told him: Alan, the box is locked but no one has thrown away the key. So I'm not lying. I never lie to him.

Complicated.

Well it wouldn't be, Anni, except that he has retreated into his shell, great tortoise that he is, to develop other, highly exclusive interests. I mean, I may have feared that young Jane at his work, but I never expected competition from the Premier League. Not from that quarter.

Well, Dan and I had better be going.

Where will you stay in the meantime?

With Dan's brother in Tufnell Park.

I can keep Cindy for you. She won't leave. She knows the area. Such a clever animal. Sometimes I think she knows things we don't. Shall I tell you a joke? Dan? You say to your cat, cat, in this case Cindy. Cindy, who is the glorious chairman of the people's revolution? Wait. Look at Cindy.

I'm looking.

Poke her.

Mao.

You see. It's an old joke. As old as any of us.

I never took you as having a revolutionary bent, Mrs F.

Oh but I do have one. Vladimir Ilýich. Che. Eminem. All very interesting to me.

What does Mr F say to that?

Him? Nothing. As I say, he's a devotee of the Premier League. He can be quite boring, actually. He would never go on holiday to Perpignan, for example. Wherever it is.

Dan didn't know where it was, either—

And you still went? A true adventurer, Dan.

We didn't want a soul to know where we were, Mrs F. Did we, Anni?

With or without Dan I had to go there some day. They say— Salvador Dali says—Perpignan train station is the centre of the world.

Oh yes, Anni, I know him. His clocks melted without any fires.

So we can't say we regret it, Mrs F. Anni and I have been to the centre of the world. The purported centre. And after all, we couldn't have put out the fire from Perpignan, even if we had known it had started when it did.

But if you hadn't gone—

If. If we start using that word we'll be here all the night.

And we have to be going, said Annabel. We have so much to do. It'll be great if you keep Cindy for the moment. Whenever you get fed up with her call.

020 8448 5621, said Dan.

One point still troubles me, Holmes, why was there no alarm? My dear Watson, why did something not happen? is often a fascinating question, don't be ashamed for asking it. So: your hypotheses, please. Well Holmes, number one, no one saw it burning. Correct, Watson: the kitchen—the seat of our fire—is at the back, the neighbours' living rooms at the front. Indeed in our day they were even called *front* rooms. The kitchen was the *back* kitchen. This simple explanation for our couple's tragedy is enshrined in our very language. A linguist, not a detective, would have been sufficiently expert to have settled this point. Sit yourself down Watson, what are you doing?

Hm, a linguist indeed. *Linguistic Inspector Watson*, how do you do. Sorry Holmes, daydreaming. Go on.

Then these televisions, Watson, root people to their armchairs as surely as any good pipe or ripping yarn. As we discovered, a person can scale a garden fence and even walk to the front without being seen or heard. So need we say more on the subject, I congratulate you on your main thrust—no one saw the fire. Such things happen, or in this case, don't happen, and so the house burned down. Now hand me my pipe. Well, Holmes, that was easy enough; and if you ask me, this *tele*vision is an enemy in itself, bloody hell. Exactly, said Holmes fixing his pipe, bloody hell.

Dan, we went on holiday and lost our house, I can't get over it. You know what I think? Those insurers may have been right with that funny theory with the cooker. Cindy stepping on the controls. I never bother pressing that safety *key*, do you?

I don't. And I wouldn't put it past her. Dancing about the hot plates. It makes you think: how technology can burn down your home.

They better pay up. Do you know how many years I spent collecting those Le Creuset saucepans? Who's going to pay me to collect that lot again? I'm so despondent. Where is your brother?

Out.

Thank God for that. But only for that. We have nothing. We don't even have a milkman any more. What was his name? So friendly until we got those broken eggs. John Wright? And what happens to all our *post* now?

I don't know. Anni—

Annabel, not Anni. I'm not an Okie, I play the piano. I was practising Beethoven's Opus 31 before we went on holiday. Why oh why did I ever marry someone whose brother has no piano?

Hm, I need time on that one, Anni.

You don't know what this is doing to me, Dan. And what about all our *bills*? What if the meters have gone haywire and we get huge bills?

With no post?

Dan, we have hit existential rock bottom.

Right. Now what?

Actually Holmes, for a moment I thought you were going to say they started this fire themselves, they didn't care for the house because they had discovered its foundations were sinking or something, and they weren't actually in Perpignan at all. Oh yes, said Holmes lighting up, we may assume they were in Perpignan. They sent you a card I expect, ho ho, said Watson, how can you be sure they were in Perpignan? Be calm, Watson, sit yourself down. The essential thing is: in their search for tranquillity, a respite from the rush and tumble of the modern world, they went on holiday anxious that no one would know where they were. But if they were planning arson, they would have done just the opposite. One of them at least would have gone, *demonstrably* gone, to the place they said they were going to, *and* have come to the telephone to receive the bad news. Or,

said Watson excitedly, they could have used this new e, e-mail.
I doubt that, said Holmes. In any case, I can't think of a criminal
so clever as to ensure he had no alibi. Would you do that,
Watson, make sure you had no alibi? I'm not that clever, no. You
see, said Holmes, you see. Now take a walk dear fellow, as I will
shortly be playing my violin.

Dan, said Annabel in their tiny room at the back in Tufnell Park,
I'm ageing. Have you noticed the way my head is sinking into my
neck? I've aged through not having received the immediate nod
from our insurers. They're putting us over more fences than
there are in the Grand National. Why did we have them? We
could have so easily gone to the Alliance.

We agreed not to, Anni, I hardly need remind you. It was
you who said: we must take a Marxist line over insurance, go for
a small firm. Shall I run you through the arguments? First, the
economies of scale achieved by the big companies—am I boring
you Anni?

It was a rhetorical question, Dan. Only you didn't spot it. And
if I yawned I'm sorry. I yawned because I can't sleep at your
brother's. Why can't he go to bed before eleven like everyone
else? Before twelve would do. But go on. Hit me with *Das Kapital*.

What's the point?

You're right. I'm off to bed. Not that it's far to go.

What are you reading?

Antonio Lobo Antunés.

Oh yeah, read him. He's good.

He is.

That's it then. Another day in paradise. And I'm going to
abandon all hope of ever getting *Das Kapital* in my Christmas
stocking. Still I can always borrow your mum's copy. Dog-eared
as it is.

Last year you got a bottle of cognac and you were pleased.

I was. I was pleased.

Which wraps things up nicely. Almost.

So are you satisfied, Watson?

Satisfied? It was a thrill—coming back on the Tube, as they call it. Racing on so madly. Even those stairs seemed to move, Holmes. Then more bedlam up above. Everyone flinging themselves in all directions. In the hurly-burly I almost failed to find our doorway. But here we are, and I must say I'm glad to be back with Mrs Hudson.

No no Watson, are you satisfied with the *case*? Oh the case. Satisfied? Not exactly, no. It all seems to have gone round in circles somehow. And the insurance paid in the end. Even though it was all rather strange, with the cat hopping on the stove and those *buttons* it seems to have pressed. *Buttons*, Holmes—words are not what they were.

My dear fellow, be not surprised by anything, least of all by what happened here.

I'll try.

Let me tell you, life is infinitely stranger than anything which the mind of man can invent. If we could just fly out of that window, hover over this great city, removing the roofs, and peep in at the queer things going on, the plannings, the cross-purposes, the wonderful chains of events, leading to the most *outré* results, it would all make fiction, with its conventions and foreseen conclusions, most stale and unprofitable. And if in this case our investigations changed nothing of substance, we at least uncovered the nuances and intricacies that beset the situation. We furthermore partook the air of another century, and was it not strange and different, albeit somehow much the same.

Yes Holmes, I don't doubt you, so I may take it you're looking forward to the next case, will you be taking us back on the Tube? Have us hurtle to some new destination. You mean the next fire, Watson. Next fire? Of course, the next of many I don't doubt. So long as there are cats and cookers, Watson, cats and cookers. But Holmes, there is one last thing that troubles me. Out with it, Watson. *How* could the Fortunes have got to Perpignan, which I understand is practically in *Spain*, stayed there, and got back, in just two weeks? Who said they did, Watson? You said so yourself. Did I, surely not? I said no criminal, no arsonist, would deliberately set himself no alibi, unless he was supremely clever. You mean? I do, Watson, I do. Like you, I know that only God or a fiction writer could have taken the Fortunes across the Channel and back in such a time. Such an obvious fact, yet no one thought to question it. So why Holmes, why did you say nothing about this before? Because, Watson, we have been talking to the supreme criminals, who left no evidence behind them. And surely we would not be so foolish as to alert them that we are on to them; but we are on to them, Mr Dan and Annabel Fortune. Wait and see, they will buy another house and we will catch them in the act, you may mark my word, we will have them next time.

To wrap things up finally. Madrid beat Arsenal on aggregate. Le Creuset shares hit a high. And Cindy will continue to a grand age. She will not chase a fly which gets trapped in an instrument panel where its eggs eventually hatch and bring down a jet in the North Sea. She lives a quiet back-garden life, staying with the Flowers and occasionally deliberating on the leader of the Chinese revolution. Mrs Flowers still recounts the afternoon she was visited by Sherlock Holmes. And that's it. The readers, mysterious participants that you are, may rest. Or try that phone number. See if you can get a good talk going or if that number's as much use as an old tea bag. Speak to Anni. Ask for Dan. Discuss the shortcomings of home insurance, Perpignan, *Das Kapital*. Have him update the whole saga in person.

Signed God and the fiction writer, 12th January 2007

History

A door has been blown down, decides Julie hurrying to Waterloo Bridge. Blasted open by Muhammed Ali and the Beatles and psychedelia and the spirit of Mao. Mary Quant and Cream and Jefferson Airplane. With the door down, a huge light, godly and joyous, has exploded onto us. Infused by the light, our hearts thrill to a common beat.

By the Shell building the sky opens at the river. O history, cries Julie enjoying herself, the sky, the spring edging into summer. Someone, it's been said, is always looking into the river near Waterloo Bridge. History: when Virginia Woolf made this remark (1915) the bridge was a different structure, said to be the noblest in the world. A hundred years it stood and stood. But (1923), holy theodolite, its piers began to sink. Ugly concrete came—and saw and conquered. It would conquer, wouldn't it. And of *course* someone is always looking into the river there. Julie probably would too, were she not anxious to reach Hungerford footbridge, climb the steps and cross the Thames there.

Not, surely, since the siege of Paris (with Edouard Manet naturally dropping his brushes to take part)—no, earlier still, not since the French Revolution, was there such a frenzy. Not since the storming of the Bastille did we quiver so, if then.

At the top of the steps a man dressed entirely in red offers her a Polaroid picture—of a dark flower he says, a poppy he says—and a packet of an unknown thing. But she hesitates on account of all she's carrying. She has books for Terry and her bag and *Purple Haze* by Jimi Hendrix tight in her hand. Already another person has the photo of the flower. Her own bootsteps thud on the walkway. There are vibrations; a crossing train roars the bridge to life. Why do people say to *lose* your virginity. Why not to *win* something else. It's a trick to try and stop you. But everyone knows a door has been blown down. Every person knows this light is on everything.

Terry says he loves her so much he would cross any bridge to reach her, be it strung through the air of a canyon, or narrow as a cheese-cutting wire. Is he saying he feels unassailably confident? That he will do things well, be gentle with her? Does she want him to do things well? She pictures him crossing a bridge on needle-thin steel beside what looks like paving but is actually nothing, it's trick paper, a hologram. Directly below this tightrope and similarly invisible, under the very skin of the surface of the Thames, glides a patrol of crocodiles, put there by the Pentagon, waiting for Terry to slip. He walks a line so straight she thinks it can't be him. Terry is too tentative, lines made by his walking would be spidery and crinkling. But the royal blue shirt with the white cuffs and collar are him. His briefcase. The yellow tie she made for him flaps stiffly towards Westminster. She should make him a purple tie. *Purple haze: all in my brain.* Terry is the only person under thirty she knows has a briefcase. He doesn't look down, he doesn't slip, he'll make it. The crocs with the stars and stripes on their thick tongues get washed down past Tower Bridge by the tide. Making for the assembly point before their long crossing to Vietnam. She stands firm and lets Terry run to her.

De-flowered, Julie does not like this either. Even Manet in his correspondence, which Julie is reading, used this word in a letter to Emile Zola. *I'm in the middle of Madeleine Férat and don't want to wait till I've finished to congratulate you. Your descriptions of the love scenes are enough to deflower any virgin who reads them.*

So we can forget the whole plan and instead of real life I can read this Férat book. What about *af*-flowered. Or just plain flowered.

Terry says the flat they're going to in Pimlico belongs to two sisters. Their place is full of smoky lamps and velvety curtains and in their dark living room they have a bronze Buddha and a chestful of costumes. What's more, says Terry, in the room we get to use, the sisters have ripped out the carpets, applied glossy orange paint to the floorboards and written *Love Shack* in wavy letters on the door. The sheets have the word *love* on them a dozen times. This is not for the benefit of her and Terry, it's simply the sisters' room. They paint wherever they go. Silver suns and jungle cats are in the hall. They've turned the bathroom blue. They are loaning their stereo speakers, which are apparently wonderful if you have a record in stereo. Jimi is mono, sorry. *Excuse me: while I kiss the sky*.

Julie sees the man in red has left red footprints.

It is a good time to be studying history. No revolutionary should be ignorant of Lenin, Vladimir Ulyanov. Or Mao, even Manet. Terry is not a revolutionary yet, but who can say that may not change. I love Terry not because he is heading the revolution but because he is a caring person who I can imagine spending Sundays lying in bed with all day. If I become his female Che Guevara he will have made his contribution. We shall be losing our virginities together. Gaining their opposites together. Adulthood sounds wrong too. Our licences. Perhaps liberty is the opposite of virginity.

They will have the flat to themselves until six in the evening. Terry says he would have preferred to be somewhere where they would spend the night together, waking to see each other. I don't care, Julie said, I just want to do it. Well right, Terry agreed, I see it that way too of course, I mean, as well as seeing it the other way. But do you want to wait? said Julie. No, he said. Because, Julie said, I've been waiting centuries already. Yes, said Terry. He had on his Carnaby Street shirt with the red roses. She kissed him. I'm thinking of growing a moustache, he said. Then I'd better kiss that part while it's still there, said Julie. Right, he said. When they kissed this time Terry put his hand in her blouse. His hand lay stock-still on her breast. When you have a moustache, Julie said, will you still have your briefcase? Yes, he said, I'll still have my briefcase. I need it. Julie ruffled his sandy hair. That's decided then, she said. What is? he said. I'll go to the advice place, she told him, as soon as I can get an appointment.

Julie overtakes Hare Krishnas waving peacock feathers. She takes a feather. Coming from the opposite direction, a group pushing cycles squeezes past. A woman gives her a leaflet. The bicycle is holy, it says, the automobile unholy. Today, Julie tells herself, is not the day to stop and discuss. But I shall spend my whole life learning, she declares assertively. Holloway will be a good place to study. (There are two Holloways, her grandmother reminded her. Be sure you go to the right one.) I can read Marx and follow Manet and all the rest on the side. History: 1967 is also the ninetieth anniversary of the trial of that Whistler man—*you are a great painter*, Manet wrote to him—and his nocturne pictures of the Thames. And what if he did fling a pot of paint in the public's face, as the accusation went? He was right to fling it. Mao would have flung it. Vladimir Ulyanov would have made a fist and cried *Yes!* Strike before you have to defend yourself. So what if his pictures weren't photographic likenesses? Whistler made the wooden arches of old Battersea Bridge stretch up psychedelically into the night. What I have painted is not a bridge, he told the prosecution, it is a *representation of moonlight*. Bravo. To research his subject he used to go out on boats in the dark, with a boatman's family, like something out of Dickens.

Manet Mao Manet Manet, she has butterflies.

Butterflies butterflies. But on seeing Terry in his shirt with the red roses, knowing he is the man sent her in the blazing light, she strides confidently past wolf whistles through the gates to the gardens.

Hello love, he greets her.

Hello, darling. Look what I've brought you, says Julie. I brought you the book about Isambard Kingdom Brunel. He has such a wonderful name.

He has? You talk as if he were alive.

That's reading. Reading does that.

You read about everything, says Terry. You're a bookworm. A bookhound.

I'm not, says Julie pretending to scowl. And if I were I wouldn't care. Do you know the chains for the Clifton suspension bridge used to cross the Thames at Hungerford Bridge?

I didn't.

Well you should, she says laughing: bridges are important things. Especially with such a big dirty old river. Without them I would have had to walk round via Oxfordshire.

I'm glad there are bridges, darling.

And they have to be crossed.

Yes.

Well I'm glad you get my point. Here's Jimi Hendrix too. *Purple haze, all in my brain. Lately things just don't seem the same.* I like that. Things have stopped being the same. They will do after today. (Everyone's in a constant state of excitement, she thinks, don't you feel it?)

Yes. Thanks.

We should go. It's a fair walk to Pimlico.

Darling, Julie.

What?

Are you quite sure you want to?

I am. I am sure. Are you not sure?

Me? I. I am.

Well that's settled, says Julie. I've got everything we need in my bag.

Very business-like.

Practical. Romantic but practical.

Right. Wait, not that way. This way. There are demonstrations over Nigeria.

Terry, stop. I want to kiss you. I love you.

I love you too, Julie. I'll always come to meet you down here.

Not always. Don't be silly.

I am silly.
You're Terry, that's all.
You're Julie.
I know I'm Julie.

Julie walks along the river with Terry, past Whistler's haunts.
Hearing sirens and seeing police vans and smoke at Westminster,
they cross the river to the Albert Embankment. Big Ben strikes
two. In the place with the door blown down are people with
transistor radios, guitars and sandwiches. On a board an outsize
copy of an advertisement from *The Times* demands marijuana be
made legal; a great roll of paper with signatures is unwinding a
hundred yards along the embankment towards Lambeth. Things
will not be the same. Britain is applying for membership of the
European Economic Community. The number of cathedrals in
Liverpool has doubled overnight. *I ain't got no quarrel with them
Viet Congs*, Muhammed Ali said refusing his country's call to
arms.

She and Terry run. By Lambeth Palace (archbishop attacked by
five hundred apprentices, 1640), her cheeks feel red, her forehead cool. She feels one moment cool, the next excited.
Trembling. Are you excited? she asks Terry. Yes, he says. That's
all: yes. Turning back north, they cross Lambeth Bridge. A wind
blows, it's hard to catch full breaths. Yes? Yes? Terry insists they
run more. Feeling her heart beating, Julie returns to a walk.
Terry starts talking about everyone who's got moustaches. Keith
Richards and Pete Townshend and Sean Connery. Julie decides
her mauve skirt needs to be turned into something more anar-
chic. She's heard it's even possible to get psychedelic underwear.
Facing drug charges that day, smiling huge smiles throughout,
Mick Jagger is wearing a sumptuously embroidered shirt and
Keith Richards elegant pinstripes. The Beatles' next record will
be called *Sergeant Pepper's Lonely Hearts Club Band*.

Seeing the street name, Julie realises it has been engraved upon
her brain for days. Tall sheets of paper have been hung across
the pavement as part of a programme of street events. Leaping

through the paper is the first event and Julie leaps through. On the other side, women are spray-painting a poem on more paper. Terry has leapt through his paper and Julie pulls him past the poem and the next event, where people are being given rear-view mirrors which are being used to flash sunlight onto a wall. Then there is a barrel of free apples and a box of penny whistles. Across the street a man is walking on his hands. The sight puts Julie fleetingly in mind of Manet's trapeze artist swinging through the top of his canvas of the Folies-Bergère. (Manet, Julie has concluded, links all things; he is the key to everything; like Shakespeare's plays, his paintings cross frontiers and time.) A very fleeting picture. Flash, it's gone. What's going on with me? she wonders. Would she have preferred to grasp her woman-hood with Manet? Manet Manet. But he had syphilis. He lived far away. History: Manet thrilled to London and would have been delighted to return, but the siege of Paris capped his plans. His one and only visit—when he wanted to meet Whistler but Whistler was away on a yacht somewhere—was made precisely one century before Julie takes off her clothes and chatters under the sheet waiting for Terry, who has forgotten to take his socks off, who has got up again and removed them, stumbling clum-sily on the orange floorboards before lying beside her all over again. For a while the power of speech seems to have left them. They lie like logs and exchange remarks about the ceiling. Actually, Julie says, I have to go to the toilet. Now that she stands, her limbs feel faint. 400,000 people have marched on the United Nations building to demonstrate against the Vietnam war. A Detroit love-in ends in a police riot. Julie comes back from the bathroom and now Terry wants to go but he has wrapped the sheet around him *love love love* so Julie hugs herself standing on the floorboards and gets distracted by photos of the sisters in a collage on the wall. They wear the shortest, tightest, gayest clothes. They have been in New York. If Julie is not mistaken they have been photographed in the King's Road with none other a person than Mary Quant.

There is a giant freakout at the London Roundhouse. A Vietnam rally is gathering in Trafalgar Square. A press release says the BBC is banning playing the Beatles' hallucinogenic *A Day in the Life*. Should this be combated? Of course. How? Manet told Degas not to disdain the Legion of Honour. *Go for everything that can set you apart from others. It's one more hurdle passed; one more weapon. We can never be too well armed for the endless battles we have to fight.* Legionnaire John Lennon MBE takes delivery of a new piano, its Romany scrolls and swirls the design of two sisters who John says live in a flatful of buddhas in Pimlico. There Julie is now taking Terry's weight and has tightened up inside in a kind of brute determination to go ahead come what may. On the Thames a pensioner returns to welcoming crowds after sailing the world single-handed. Julie feels Terry hurting her but she will go through with it, he doesn't mean to hurt her. He is a good man even if he cannot part himself from his briefcase, despite his sparse ways of communicating. There is day-long music at the Golden Gate Park in San Francisco, protests at the London School of Economics. America is found guilty in Vietnam at the Russell Tribunal in Stockholm. Will she ever find out a single thing about the sex lives of the sisters? Do Hare Krishnas have (good) sex lives? The sun is shining through the window, the room is no longer cold. Terry has a pretty burst of freckles on one shoulder. Close by in London, gold bars are stolen from a van in the biggest robbery of its kind. At evening time people queue to see *The Graduate*; by day the publishers of the allegedly obscene book *Last Exit to Brooklyn* go to trial. In Paris huge numbers of people protesting against the United States in Vietnam are arrested. Julie thinks of the records that are going up the charts. Jimi Hendrix, the Move, the Kinks, the Who, and at number one that mesmerising wedding hymn from Bach. Terry: at first just ghosting, as in the hymn, has turned a whiter shade of pale. His clothes and hers are scattered on the floor. To move things on, she asks him to fetch a towel from her bag. She won't hold anything that's happened against him. Julie tells herself they have to do this, sex, making love, love not war, exchanging virginity for liberty, any way they can. Only then, she decides, will they be able to do it better.

Tender

Things were different then, as we authors are fond of saying: and they were the same. The Vietnamese were being napalmed while we drank instant coffee and played our twelve-string guitars. Some of us had dulcimers. Still others knew what a dulcimer was.

In a tiny dim-lit, candle-lit sixth floor *appartement* in the seventh arrondissement of Paris, producing the tenderness they will carry with them closely, as all tenderness is carried closely, incommunicable to others, until it is lost for ever at the grave, are Natacha Finn Bréchet (diplomat's daughter), who just this moment said *à fleur de peau*, and US boy Jay Rosenthal, who seconds earlier (we only just missed it) put back on his white T-shirt (barely legible writing to be revealed the moment he turns to the light).

Natacha is lying back looking towards the ceiling, her greatest glory, her platinum-blonde hair spread everywhere.

Affler? Afflerdupoe? says Jay, sitting up with his back to her. He turns to her suddenly (UNION C *Glit*).

On the surface, says Natacha reaching up at his cheek (*douce, douce*). *A fleur de peau, peau* is skin and so you get: not even skin-deep. Just touching *la surface*. Like this. *A fleur de peau.*

If it's like that, boy it's all right with me, says Jay (UNION CITY *Glittering on the Hudson*, dark writing over faded pink tie-dye).

His interest in making love revives. He takes his T-shirt back off and pushes her legs apart. *Mais non*, says Natacha. Drawing heavily on films for her English, she says Americanly: *Come on, Mr Rosenthal, you can do better than that.*

How are things meanwhile in Union City, New Jersey? While it is dark in the seventh arrondissement, and the night is trying to fill the Seine with its darkness, is daylight indeed glittering on the Hudson? No? How about metaphorically? Well, the mother of Jay, Kay Rosenthal, is deeply in trouble. Disturbingly in trouble. Let the author take a break, go for a walk, while she communicates her disturbance her own way.

My son Jay amuses himself over in Europe, in the moment Paris. In order to escape the draft, design, the draft, he cannot return. But they will after him go. Until I know what should become of him I will remain locked in the bathroom. I know what I make, I am not displaced. I can tell crazy things but that does not displace me crazy. It's true: in a flea market in Madrid you could buy a canary in a paper paper bag. This not displace me, it is a fact. So I will remain here. I got all I need. Out of the window I get to see a tall strip of clapboard. Maybe some time Alice or Becky will walk by it. Inside I got everything from magazines to a pair of shears. Cases of Briar's, birch beer, sarsaparilla—what the heck are they doing here? Some empty notebook and a pen. Hell, I can write my memoirs.

I am backing off, I will explain to my married man through the keyhole. Kay, he'll say, only he doesn't say Kay much. From Kay he moved to K, which he said is potassium, he had chemistry in school. From potassium to Tass. You can call me Al, he said, or if you like Aluminium; that way we are two silvery metals. Complicated? No way. He's as straight as can be. Aluminium is a service facility, works mainly at Union City Chemicals supplying snacks and drinks and maintaining embarrassment incorrect gadgets.

How come he's back already, I hear the red car in the roadway of the window. I am of the people who can hear colours. We had pink and blue cars and we have now cherry red, and that is him. I hear very silvery fenders. Him. Out of one door, shut, and through the next door, shut, soon he'll be at this door. "Tass," he's calling, "Tass." He's rattling and rattling the doorknob. And what does he say? "Tass," he sighs, "goddamn."

Aluminium leans his ear at the jump in the door and hears for an answer. I'm pretty sure that's what's happening. I hear only raspy the tones of him outside breathing. I go to look through the hole and nearly stick the key through my eye. I rattle the door to make it sound like I'm relocking it while actually I'm taking out the key so I can look through better. Although it gives nothing to see. I see a check of reddy-blue shirt, a lump where he keeps some kind of pen in his pocket. "You leave Kay to me," says he and I turn back the key, then I go round and back a few ways.

Silence. Murmur-urmur.

"Aluminium? What's that yakking back there? Don't pretend you're talking to someone."

"OK."

"No persons in this universe would get me shooting out of here. Jay is about the only one. Do you have Robert Redford out there?"

"Yep. Robert Redford. Just called by with Paul Newman. Gone out without hats. Thought they could borrow a coupla hats. I said I'd ask you."

"Tell 'em that's OK. Tell 'em I'll meet them another time maybe."

"OK. Now open up Kay. I want the beverages. Alice and Steve got no Briar's. Aw, come on, Tass."

"Aw come on yourself. How come you're home now?"

"I came for the game. So I can get things ready first. I want you out. This is the third time this week. We got a whole house you can hide in, why you gotta go for the bathroom?"

"It says on this pack: We will never stop listening to our customers' suggestions. I got one: Leave me be."

"I need the Briar's. You read on down what you're reading—"

"We will try to get our soft drinks into your hands no matter how far you are from the nearest distribution point."

"That's me. Let me in. I gotta distribute."

I do love Aluminium. My distribution point. The hell to all that, he's out to trick me. I love him and I love him and I don't trust him. Do I doubt in him? Sure I do. Why. Oh boy, here we go again, go questioning. What is there about him? How come I'm in a house with him? I look to see if that piece of shirt is still there. It's a different piece. I try picturing more of him. I press a button inside: Aluminium, a moving picture please. There he is. He shuffles when he walks—

"Are we having a fight, Kay? Is that what this is?"

That's all the objections I can think up. Hell, it wasn't a lot. It was hardly none at all. I love Aluminium dear.

"You come out, Tass," he says, "I'm staying here until you come out."

His inhaling is sharp, it could cut through steel. It may cut round the lock so he can put his hand through. He just blows a circle around the lock and it falls clunk into the bathroom. I put a hand over the spot, to hold it there, just in case.

Nothing happens.

I stay sat on the floor. I feel my cheeks. They feel raspy. I look to see if I can find a place on my head my fingers have never been. I go questioning one more time. I end up at our boy. Where is our boy? I go closer still to the door. "Hey," I say softly, into the jump.

"Hey. Hey what?"

I hear myself sigh by the keyhole. "I sent him his T-shirt and what does he send back? Nothing. Union City, Glittering on the Hudson. *I* wrote it on myself. I *wrote* it. Supposed to be indelible. Is it glittering there now?"

"How the goddamn heck should I know? The Hudson's goddamn blocks away. We got offices and warehouses and tyre stores and a refrigeration plant in the way, remember? You want I tear down a whole bunch so you can check out a coupla bathtubs of beat-up old water?"

"I'm staying until I know he's all right."

"Please yourself. I could get you out of there in a flash if I wanted. I got so many ways I could get a prize for thinking of them."

"From who? Prize from who?"

"Let me tell you something, Tass. Tonight there's a special on the '62 floods. Seven years ago this weekend. But if you come out for that you'll be sicker than one of those paper-bagged canaries you're always telling me of."

"I'd be sick. Maybe we better watch it, though."

"They'll upset you, what with your cousin lying dead on the dike like you said. Though you only met the kid twice."

I'll be silent. Have a silence start stretching out. I'll be a ship disappeared in the fog.

Aluminium has his ear to the jump. "Tass, you hardly knew him."

"I know, but I just took him to heart."

"Anyways, better stay where you are."

"You don't care if I'm in here or out there."

"Right, I don't care."

"Don't care!"

"Of course I care, Tass! I care, I care, I care."

"I'm coming out."

"That's it, good girl, there you go now. Don't forget there's the game on tonight too. The Giants and the Browns."

"You think I care? You think I care about your goddamn games? What about our boy? That's what I care about."

"Honey, he'll be dancing the night away at the old Folly Ber-jer. Sure, sure, he'll be throwed into some dungeon by noon and under the guillotine by sundown. And dressed the whole time in nothing but an old beyrey, OK?"

"What the hell is that?"

You want me? says Natacha, then you have to be *actif*. Not like that, we are not doing a sport.

Tache, says Jay. That's what I wanna call you: Tache. My dad—

I will tell you what you do. So that I *trombull*.

Tremble, says Jay. You want to?

Of course, everybody want to tremble.

I had another question. I forgot it. Must have lost it some-where. Maybe it's under here, you got it under here? That tickle?

All right all right.

Well all *right*.

All right, maybe you do things differently in Union City. In France we want to tremble.

Like when Napoleon's coming? Napoleon's coming, going to eat our babies. I heard someone say that.

So first, you go like this. You touch—no, not like that. Like this. Then you go across. Not prefer one and not the other, you understand. Do you understand?

Like so?

And you concentrate. I have the impression you are somewhere else, you have some problem. What is your mind on?

My mother is crazy.

Really? Really crazy?

I think so.

A dulcimer is a kind of zither, which may be struck with hammers or plucked. Then there is the *gimbri* or *guinbri* (a small north African lute). Robin Williamson of the Incredible String Band played it with a bow, wrenching melancholy chords of unearthly beauty. A virtuoso, he could equally play talking drums or pick up the Chinese banjo. Fairport Convention simply had Dave Swarbrick playing the violin. A Great Dane slept on stage as Fairport performed *If I had a ribbon bow to tie in my hair* with Judy Dyble and others, Martin Lamble at the drums, Richard Thompson on guitar. Or perhaps the Great Dane came later. Later: when dogs slept to inimitable Sandy Denny singing, for want of a less neutral word, singing, moving hearts by the thousands.

I never had said let's go to the Palisades, I just along the river street to us. That's OK. Now I can see at least for me even. Therefore glitzern no large business, it glitzert generally not exactly however I am satisfied here. We only can sit and can regard the skyline, hope only that our boy may regard the skyline each time he wants the skyline to regard. Each time in his long life.

"We coulda taken a ride down the shore but this is the spot you wanted, Jeez. OK, if it is then do me a favour too, don't do that again in the bathroom, OK?"

"OK. I'm glad we're here, it's almost romantic."

"This beat-up old parking lot? This scrag chicken run is part of a film no one reconned for first, unless it was a recce for a B52, and now we gotta make the most of a whole lotta nothing and an old river no one but your canary in a paper bag might appreciate a look at."

"It reminds me of our honeymoon."

"Tass are you are off your head, since when did we sit opposite Universal Folding Box on our honeymoon, come on. See next to that buncha bulldozers, they're gonna make a recreation park out of that, one of these days. Then it might work coming here. At least we could get a beer someplace. An Italian hot dog. Lotta onion, I could picture it."

"You never told me there was going to be a recreation park here."

"I'm telling you."

"Why didn't you tell me before?"

"Before what? Jeez, I'm telling you."

"Being by the river takes me back to our honeymoon."

"So you said. Except we weren't by no river. There was one river, and that was just one afternoon, a little trip we made, and that was next to a practice ground for some tanks."

"You remember that, honey? I'm so pleased."

"Yeah, well I'm pleased you're pleased. At least the skyline looks good. If only it weren't so far away. New York, New York."

"I was peroxide and you were such fun, Aluminium. Whoever would have had the idea of a honeymoon on the middle of a moor. You were such fun."

"So you keep saying. So I'm not any more? Wonderful, wonderful."

"You remember you went out in the dark to look for a phone."

"Yeah, yeah, goddamn phone in the dark. Goddamn English phone box with donkeys—

"Ponies."

—ponies staring through in the dark, wanting to chomp through the phone book. I don't know nothing about no ponies on no moors, or a whole buncha them couldn't wait to dial some urgent call to some pony somewhere. Couldn't wait to hold the receiver in their teeth. I was lucky to get out of that box alive."

"What did we call that place, Widdecombe in the Moo."

"Yeah, Widdecombe in the Moo. Come here, Tass."

Jay Rosenthal takes a pocket dictionary from his backpack and crawls on his elbows over to the candle. Union City Glittering on the Hudson is swallowed by the dark, as if on the far side of the moon.

A fleur de peau. I'll try *fleur* first. *Flame, fleur, fleurette.* Natacha, he says, *je te conte fleurette.* I am flirting with you.

C'est bien possible, says Natacha, but no one says *conter fleurette* any more.

It's pretty though.

That's not enough. To be pretty.

I think you're pretty.

Thank you. If I am I am. *Je suis belle donc je suis.*

Huh? Do you want to go out somewhere?

I like it here. With you. The candles.

This place is neat. That weird heater, the bookshelf down by the floor, that curtain round the sink. It reminds me of something. The mirror there must be the littlest mirror—

It's just a place when girlfriends stop over.

That's very good English, Tache: when girlfriends stop over. Could be a film. *When Girlfriends Stop Over.*

You have a girl in Union City?

I—hey, you aren't supposed to be asking questions like that.

So it is yes. What is her name?

I—let's change the subject.

No, I want this subject. I do not care if you have a girl there, she is not here, what is her name?

Er—well.

Yes?

Debbie.

Debbie.

Debbie. Debbie from Union City too. We haven't made each other promises. We're not engaged. So like you say, Tache, it doesn't matter.

I have a boyfriend in England. He is a student at the university. But he is not here, either.

So you've—learned English from him.

Not really. Not very much.

Tache, I don't know what to do now, I find it hard to keep going like we have.

You find it difficult? I will make it easy. I can tell you, there is another reason I use this room. Look.

Jesus. Three already rolled.

Oui. You want? Afterward we refresh *la pièce* a lot.

How do we do that, there's no windows.

There is one, behind you. And we burn these sticks. *Attention.* Keep your hair from the candle. Here.

Thanks. Thanks, Tache. Now what?

Come here. It is my turn, I will perform. You will be still. You do nothing. It will be good. Very good. You will remember, when you take your train at *la Gare de l'Est demain.* You want? You will.

For hours the storm had raged over the North Sea, its powerful north-westerlies forcing high water into the mouth of the Elbe. In the port of Hamburg the water level was rising higher and higher, an imminent flood was unstoppable. In the night of 16 to 17 February the sea eventually reached the top of dikes that protected the city. The floods tore holes in their green lines.

"Our dike broke in two places. Immediately the water swept up in waves. We knew the water was high, it had got higher each night for two nights, but we had dikes. We weren't worried because that's what the dikes are for—

"Jesus look at that."

"Don't show us bodies."

"We had pigs then. All the pigs were swept away, along with—

"How come they're speaking English, Aluminium?"

"You think I know?"

"You think it's dubbed over the top of them?"

"There was a pile of shit too, it floated out with the pigs."

"Maybe."

"You can't tell?"

"The outhouse was smashed. The funny thing was—

"OK honey, just let me switch to my in-depth investigatory-ing self. OK, if you look at their lips, *look there*, look look, they don't move right. I reckon they *know* we're looking at it knowing it's not really them speaking. But it's their words."

"How can it be their words if they're not speaking?"

—one pig lay on top of the pile of shit. And what became of it? It was the only one that survived."

"Goddamn, Tass, you want a beer too? The game's on in three minutes."

"Would you thinka lying on a pile of shit if you were a pig? Would you do it?"

"Sure."

"Say you were a person—

"Well OK, thanks, yeah I'll try."

"And it was people's shit. Would you lie on it then?"

"Hm. Hell, no. I'd be pretty careful to swim round it."

"I looked out of the window and the fields that had always been fields were water. All that was missing was for a freighter to sail past. The moon was bright and we could see everything. Like I said, all it needed was a freighter, and then the plumber's van comes floating by."

"They sorta made it entertaining. I don't think you need to worry about seeing any bodies anywhere."

"First it was all that water out there, then suddenly we were part of it. It was so big, it was terrifying. People died terrified. We heard them cry for help, we even saw them sometimes, but there was nothing we could do."

"OK I take that back about the entertaining. Are you still really wrapped up in it Tass?"

"I guess—I guess not, not like I was. I got Jay to worry about now."

"No way is our boy in some flood. Even if he was, he's like you. He'd lie on the shit."

"I never said I'd lie on the shit."

"You would though. Because you have to be there for your boy. You have to stay alive, whatever it costs."

"I went downstairs just before the lights went out and the sofa caught fire, some kind of short circuit. I tried to put it out with water and the electric shock threw me back up the stairs."

Only the survivors are there to tell the tales. Sea water engulfed the district around the port. 20,000 people lost everything they had. Three hundred and forty died.

"You cry all you want, honey. So long as you wind down for the game. If the Giants win this one, and they should, they'll be right on top there. And stay out of the bathroom when you don't need it for those bathroom reasons. There, now then. There is nothing in the whole goddamn world we or anybody could have done that day."

"It's such a hard world. Don't leave me alone, Aluminium. Don't leave me alone."

"Honey I told you haven't I? You can rock this boat all you want. It ain't ever going over."

The storm tide of 1962 signalled the dangers had clearly been underestimated, and the time had come to take action. Since then the dikes are being raised and straightened; flood gates and barriers are being expanded. The work will go on for some time to come.

You see. That was not anywhere in your expectations, Mr Rosenthal, *n'est-ce pas*?

Nowhere. Paradise was not on my schedule.

Every day is new. Last week you had no idea this day would be this way.

Careful, the rug.

There. I put it out with my hand. You were where, this time last week? You were with Debbie in Union City?

Take it, you got it? No, I was—in Liverpool.

Ah, *les Beatles*.

Sort of. I saw Paul McCartney's brother.

Jay, close to the stars.

He's just a normal guy, a smart guy. Or what do you mean? You making fun of me?

Natacha strokes his cheek close to his freckles, says: You are my lover now. Jay, beautiful Jay.

Jay holds her hand to his face, says: He was reading poetry. Paul's brother. Mike?

Alors?

People don't do that. They certainly don't in Union City.

I see. There is no poetry in Union City, my lover.

Yes. No. Yes. I mean—

You are so funny. You want me again now?

You can be pretty direct, Tache.

It's all right. I stroke your hair now. The hair of my lover, Mr Rosenthal. You tell me poetry now. It is the moment.

Jay.

I like Mr Rosenthal, it is fun.

They are all reading poetry to each other there, the whole time. They have been for years, they say. In those pubs and outside and on the ferry. God, reading poems.

Like in China. I think. What was in their poems? Love, sex?

Everything. Poetry is about anything, I guess. There was a poem about the Mersey Tunnel, that's a tunnel under the river with lots of bends.

You tell me.

Another poet had one about parks. It went something like. O you mighty river, squares, gardens and cathedrals, you shops and pubs and doorways are second to none. You parks with your soft animal fields, Victorian riverside earth—it's coming back to me—dinosaur parks cleared of brontosauruses, of people, emptier than ever, empires of grass, dark rainy airs, public tennis courts where I long to chase your masterful topspin lobs, to return your sweet volleys, grey air over the green grass, ancient trees, a boating lake for us to try out with our parasols and paraphernalia, listen, on Friday night you and I will go back to my ranch between my cathedrals, or hide in the mazes, behind the botanic gardens, playing that game until we are both as immovable as flower petals fallen from vases painted by Gustave Courbet and I know we are second to none.

C'est terrrible!

Jay strokes her hair from the roots to the ends; cups an ear in his hand.

Will you go with me tomorrow, Natacha?

Only to Liverpool.

Give me a break, I'm headed south.

Only Liverpool. Do you think I would hear what you just told me?

You'd hear it I'm sure. It got read five or six times, one after the other. People were clapping and stomping and going out of their heads and getting ready to blow the roof off. That's second to none, they shouted. Second to none.

That was the name of the poem?

No, replies Jay, the poet said it wasn't called that.

No? You sweet boy.

He said: it might be second to none, but I call it Tender.

Shingle Street

On a Suffolk beach I met the captain of the world's first submarine. In green oilskins he marched towards me along a stretch of golden shingle. He seemed to come from nowhere. He hadn't: I was simply not looking his way. I had been engrossed by the sight of strangely mesmerising North Sea currents, sending water surging in and out of what looked like a lagoon.

In impressive English the captain said the submarine, that designed by the Spaniard Isaac Peral, had gone aground in shingle. He said it was around the corner, behind the Martello tower to the south.

The complexion of the captain of the world's first submarine was grey and blue and blotchy, as might be expected of someone habitually shut up in deep water. Serious and solemn, he adjured me to keep the presence of the vessel and its crew a secret. I agreed, not because I believed him but because I saw no immediate problem in agreeing. He told me he commanded the real thing, famous for its flawless trials of 1889 in the Bay of Cadíz.

We were standing in one of the world's forgotten places, Shingle Street. Forgotten by people, by trees and sizeable animal life, and so by time itself.

It did not therefore seem strange that he should speak to me at length, and present the historical background to his sudden appearance. In a plot set in motion by Isaac Peral himself, the submarine had been appropriated in vengeance at the unappreciative naval authorities of the day, who wanted outrageous changes made to his design. If I cared to know the background, the captain said, Alfonso de la Pezuela, his great-grandfather and Isaac's righthand man, had switched the original for a 77-ton replica in 1914, as the great submarine was on its way to being mothballed in Cartagena. Charged with transporting the marvel, Señor de la Pezuela and his team of nine had made the switch in a cove close by Cadíz. The replica was taken on to Cartagena where, at his great-grandfather's orders, its hull was filled with cement so that it would not budge again (the cementing, carried out by night, was a further act of vengeance). The replica did move once, said the captain, although that was of no relevance to anything. It had been to Seville and back for a show, full of concrete and not the real thing. Now the impostor was back on stilts, on a plinth of cement with jets of water playing on its belly, on a forlorn esplanade in Cartagena.

He was sure I would not tell. Thousands upon thousands knew but had not told that the *Isaac Peral*, which he and the crew called *el cigarre*, had been travelling the coasts of Europe and North Africa for the best part of a century. Why had it? I asked. He took a sheet of paper from his jacket. In English were the ten questions most often asked him.

1. Why are you doing this?
   Because it is fun.
2. Why is it fun?
   There is a mission that makes it fun. The mission is to see that the whereabouts of the *Isaac Peral* do not become public knowledge.
3. But why is the boat not discovered?
   Because no one is looking for it.
4. How is it people nonetheless do not find out about what you're doing?

They do find out. But they do not tell. That would end the fun, and they respect that.

5. How do you survive?

By research. We are experts at research. We research every place we want to go to. We find the inaccessible coves. We find the people who will help us with food and repairs and supplies.

6. Who are the crew?

We are ten men, all relatives of the original ten men. We are not allowed to leave the submarine. We have chosen this life. The only other condition in selecting us is our height. Tall people are not suitable for submarines.

7. What happens to a crew member when he gets sick or old?

Doctors must come on board. If a crew member is too sick or too old he is replaced by a son or another in his family.

8. So there are no women?

No. The rules were made in 1914 and will not alter.

9. Isn't it strange to be on your way for weeks at a time and have only sporadic contact to the outside world?

Perhaps. We are old fashioned. We know this. But we keep up with technical developments because our research has to be the best. Recently, we were donated a laptop notebook. For that is our secondary mission, you might say: perfection in research.

10. How far can you travel?

396 kilometres at three knots, 284 at four knots, 132 at six knots.

He took back the paper. Now in its fifth edition, it was for information, not for copying. Having to photocopy papers ashore, he said without elaborating, had on occasions placed the crew in awkward situations. He said he would enjoy practising his English with me. He had been studying it ever since he had acquired an English grammar near Gibraltar. I put to him further questions. His name too was Alfonso, like his great-grandfather and *compadre* of Isaac Peral. Isaac had had many grudges against the government. He did not want *el cigarre* to be museumed like a stuffed steel animal. Hence the idea of the replica. The switch was extremely difficult to engineer, in every sense of this word. The *Isaac Peral* was 22 metres long and had a beam of 2.87 metres. In English these figures were 71 feet by nine.

We strolled on, towards the white coastguards' cottages for which the hamlet of Shingle Street is best known, insofar as it is known at all. There customs officials worked and lived, I warned him, but he was unworried. Did he not miss his family? I asked. Yes, he said. That was the price. Everything had its price.

What about sex? I said. Sex? he said, as if hearing of an invention he might have missed. Women, I said. He got out another sheet of paper with English words. Women, I said, *wimin*, an unphonetic word. *Mujeres*, I tried in Spanish. Ah, ah, he said. We have no, *no tengo*.

Dressed in the same oilskin green, another man came up almost running, his presence announced by the *chatch chatch* on the shingle. Ah Ramón, said the captain—who abruptly turned his attention to the water skating across the shoals, the same seascape he had caught me observing—*diga las cosas al este hombre*, talk to this man, Ramón, I must study the North Sea one moment. *Sí capitán*, said Ramón saluting before adapting this salute to flick back a great flap of hair. The mid-length style of his hair minded me of the 1970s. He asks about women, said the captain. *Mujeres*.

Ramón and I walked slowly. We are ten men, señor, he said. So sometimes we go and find women. Except Oscar. Oscar is our chief navigator, although probably the youngest such in the whole of Spain. We have him not because he is good at navigating, he is not good, we have him because his family threw him out. He wants men, there are always men who want men. He wants us too, most of us, but he cannot have us. Oscar has to wait, like the rest of us.

The captain's footsteps trudged up in the shingle.

Do you know women here? said Ramón to me under his breath.

Women? I whispered back. I don't.

What? said Ramón. I can't hear you.

I don't know a soul, I said loudly, I'm not from round here. I'm just here for a conference. A conference on tree care.

Care? Care? said Ramón.

The captain joined us.

Good, he declared without specifying what he was referring to. I hope your questions have been answered. Ramón speaks English well, indeed we all do. We have nightly spelling bees.

We made *chitch chotch* sounds as we headed for the tiny café besides the cottages. A chill gust accompanied us, causing us to pull our coats more tightly, as a front of dark and powerful clouds moved up majestically from the south.

I bid the captain sit at the only table, but Ramón stood staring at the TV behind the counter. I glanced at the screen: a lady on all fours was scrubbing at a paw-marked kitchen floor.

Women! said Ramón expectantly.

Hardly had we reached at the menus when two men in official caps walked in. Are you officers of the customs? the captain asked. Indeed, they said. The captain explained his difficulties with the submarine while immediately handing them the paper with the questions and the answers. We have nothing to declare, he added. He turned to the counter and ordered three teas.

Are you from the institute? one man asked the captain.

I have told you, he replied.

It was my turn to be given a questioning look.

I'm out walking, I said. I'm attending a conference of foresters at Snape.

I know, he said. You still have your badge on, Mr Squires.

Meanwhile Ramón kept out of the way, twirling a stand of postcards with towns along the Suffolk coast.

If you really have a submarine round the corner, the other said finally, it will almost certainly float off with the next tide. As submarines do. I suppose you have engines. You are bound to have engines.

Of course. Two electrical motors each with thirty horses' power. Six hundred and thirteen batteries. Two propellers.

Three, Ramón interposed.

All right, three, said the captain. Two vertical propellers and one horizontal. We now have a spare propeller on board as well. Please give me my paper back. Thank you.

If, the man repeated at the door.

They left.

If? said the captain to me.

A treasured English word, I said, *if*. We even have a poem called that.

I have not heard of that, said Alfonso puzzled. *Tú*, Ramón?

No.

Our country is nonetheless full of poems, Alfonso remarked.

Not *nonetheless*, corrected Ramón, *however*.

They did not believe you, I said. So I don't know what they will be thinking.

No, the captain agreed. But if they are right about the tide, all we can do is wait. But I think they know nothing about submarines.

I must have this card to send to my mother, said Ramón. It is called "the house in the clouds". Look. She will not believe this building.

Well good luck, I said.

You are not going? said Alfonso.

I should. I have a seminar. It's several miles by car.

Ramón stopped the postcards twirling, his hand on a black-and-white photo of what I guessed was Benjamin Britten. You have a *car*, señor, he said desperately.

Wait, said the captain. Do you not want to see our great ship? Our pride? I know it is not at its best, resting as it is, *beached*. But you will not have this chance one other time. You can ask the other woodsmen for their notes. Like in the school. But you cannot see the *Isaac Peral* again. We don't dock in the same place twice.

We are not docking, Ramón commented. We misjudged the currents.

It was a complicated situation Ramón. You cannot imagine, señor, he said to me, how difficult manoeuvring through the oilfields is.

Oscar, Ramón remonstrated, Oscar is to blame. Oscar was looking at pictures of men instead of his tables, I saw him. His tables were upside down.

Yes, yes, said the captain. Let us not go through that again. So you do not want to see . . . the very deck where the queen of Spain, Maria Cristina, once walked and stood . . .

No. Well yes, I said hesitantly. It would be interesting, of course. Highly . . . An extraordinary vessel. And you being captain, but . . .

I see. It is for you to choose, señor Squize. Off my back is no skin.

But I really should go.

Yes, you are leaving. Goodbye. You will keep this secret.

Oh yes.

Adios.

I left. The North Sea was still sluicing back and forth across the shoals. Short sharp waves crowded on each other's backs. I looked left and right, taking in the strange beauty of the shore called Shingle Street. No soul was in sight. The sky was closed with the cloud from the south. It started raining. I looked back to the little café. Ramón waved from inside. He beckoned frantically. He came out *chatching* fast.

Please, señor. I do not know how to say this. We men are with ourselves all the time, we need, I need . . .

He pulled out a map.

What about this place? he said. *Ipswich*.

I drew a blank and said: You got me there.

Got me? *Las chicas?* He looked up at me hopefully.

I said I didn't know.

Please come back, señor. Talk to our *capitán* Alfonso, *el pobre*. Please.

I agreed, I don't know why.

Despite the vast empty acreage of the beach, he stepped aside. After you, he implored.

The captain, whose complexion had darkened in the meantime, as if taking on the light and darkness of the weather beyond the window pane, looked up astonished. He had two charts spread across the table.

Yes?

Yes, I replied, not knowing exactly what this meant.

He rolled the charts together. And please, he said, you will call me Alfonso.

I sat back down and ordered more tea. I offered to pay for Ramón's postcard. Ramón said he would have to go back for his address book. Wait, Alfonso said.

Alfonso suggested we play some hands of Bézique to fill the time.

The time?

The time the crew would need to make things properly ship-shape for a visitor, of course.

And Bézique?

It was a favourite of his great-grandfather's. I had no idea how to play, but he sent Ramón to fetch the cards. This game is not so difficult, he said. After a month or two you can maybe win. It is my joke. Go go, Ramón, go. And take the charts. And salute.

Salute? said Ramón. I've done that once already. Salute your-self. Adios. And remember my question, señor. If you can. *If.*

Go! After we play, I take you and show you the *Isaac Peral*. We are so proud of him. In any case we are rid of Ramón now. That Ramón, much stupidness.

I voiced the notion that the captain might be glad to get away from the whole of the crew.

They are good men, he said. I would trust them with my life. I would trust them with the world's first submarine.

There was the sound of more scrunching steps.

It was Oscar, not Ramón.

Why did Ramón not bring the cards?

Blond, young, his dark blond eyebrows prominent, Oscar broke down in tears and set his head on the table.

Come on, said Alfonso. This is no good.

They are so cruel to me, Oscar said, they say I must go. Ramón says he cannot go backwards and forwards all day, he is not a delivery boy. I must go. I must run fast along the stones or they will throw them at me. I have no friends on the *Isaac Peral*. He knows? he added suddenly as he became aware of me.

Yes he knows. He is coming to see *el cigarre*.

You are from here, señor? I want to stay here. I have my passport with me. I want asylum in the United Kingdom.

Pst! said Alfonso, that is not possible. Asylum asylum, wherever we go all I hear is asylum. If you stay, we all go under. Collect yourself.

Blond Oscar sighed loudly, took out his passport and looked at the first page.

Can I stay and watch you play?

You may, said the man who told me he was the captain of the world's first submarine. It may not be so interesting for you: I shall win and win. Here are the cards, señor. I know all the English terms. Royal marriage, sequence, double bézique, ten for the seven, ten for the last trick. These are points, these tens, this is why we have these scorers that go round and round. They are very beautiful, are they not? See how this purple is set against this yellow. Such a sense of colour. You know our Velázquez.

You don't mean Velázquez, interrupted Oscar. You are crazy, he said for my benefit. Ramón says we are a team of crazies. *El equipo crónico*. Read this paper and tell me what you make of us, he said handing me a paper like the one Alfonso had.

Ramón Ramón, said Alfonso angrily.

Look at this photograph señor, said Oscar back with his passport. Do you think it looks like me?

By now the captain had the table filled with upturned cards. A double bézique, he said presenting two queens of spades and two jacks of diamonds. This is the best you can get—five hundred points. *Quinientos*, as they say on the Canary Islands. Yes there are two packs. Very beautiful. We cut. Now I cut. The king of hearts. I deal.

It is impossible to know if I was fortunate with the cards, or if the captain had over-reached himself, but he lost the series to two thousand points. Alfonso turned on Oscar. I told you, he said to Oscar, we should have stayed in the oilfield until we had a sensible plan. I am not the *capitán*, retorted Oscar, I advise but you decide, you are Alfonso de la Pezuela. Go leave me, he said to Oscar, may the dirt of birds fall on your head. Oscar agreed to go out and study the North Sea waves. But talk to no one, he ordered.

Alone again, Alfonso wanted a second series, this time to two thousand five hundred. I want to see the *Isaac Peral*, I said trying to turn our talk in that direction. According to this sheet of paper shown me by Oscar, I said, the vessel could only accommodate a crew of six, not ten.

No, ten, said Alfonso as he flicked the thousands pointer on his score card round and round. It says this but this is not true.

Look on the paper. Don't you want to see for yourself?

I know this paper. Why should I want to see it again?

Does it have a periscope?

Of course.

What about this, *a chemical system to oxygenate the air*?

Yes. Please deal. Like I said, first two cards, then three, then two again. Eight.

Three torpedoes.

No no. No torpedoes. Not any more. Not since 1914. They are in cement at the end of the esplanade the *Paseo de Alfonso XII*. We put them in our replica and hoped one day the hot sun would blow up the *paseo*. I am joking. We are strictly peace-loving. The Soviet authorities know we are there but they know we are peace-loving and they leave us.

They are not called Soviet now, I told him.

No? He shrugged. It is on account of such strategies, he resumed, we can continue our mission. It is your turn to pick up a new card. You cannot hope to do well without eight cards to play from. Ah, my trick again. Yes, we are peace-loving. Isaac was a naval officer but he turned his back on the navy. We do not consort with navies, defence departments. The *military-industrial complex*, he said pleased with the expression. We are not going to sink anyone's fleet. You keep your Francisco Drake. *Mira!*, if we had not been peace-loving we would not have agreed to be shown on our Spanish postage stamps.

You negotiated with the post office?

The Peral Post Stamp. That was a long time ago.

But the Americans must know of you too.

I don't believe so. I explain something. There are fish who make mistakes. The barracuda sees your shiny wristwatch and thinks that is a lovely swarm of fish, I must eat that. The shark swims under you and sees you with your surfboard. He thinks that is a lovely seal, I must eat that. Now America sees our submarine and says, that is a wreck, a whale, a piece of oil rig. The shark: the shark bites and tries out what he sees. Bites a bit, then he notices this seal is horrible, so he stops. Do the Americans, however? No, they don't. They don't check, they are so sure they are right. They are the shark who does not check. Don't you agree, Oscar?

Oscar's gone. You sent him out. Perhaps he's gone back on board?

Of course, how stupid, the captain said, I'm so used to having him around. They're always there, all the time. Oscar has his boo-hoo, boo-hoo, every time boo-hoo and then it's over; *Isaac* is his home. Asylum! Ah, the ace of spades. Very valuable indeed. Look, I play the nine of spades. You cannot take that, you would be stupid to take that. I win the trick and I get the ace for my seven. You see how it works. A most beautiful game. Oscar should not have given you his paper. I am afraid I must confiscate it. You will give it to me, please?

After we have gone to the ship.

Very well. After this series we shall go.

The tide is advancing, I pointed out.

Yes, he said. Four aces. A hundred points. You will not catch me this time. Where is your forest?

Losing the second series, Alfonso left the café brooding. The rain held off. The shingle was still golden although the sky was overcast. Listen, I said with a hand to one ear, the stones are moving at the mouth of the lagoon. It is not a lagoon, said Alfonso, it is a river. We discussed the movements of the local coastline. I told Alfonso about Dunwich, its medieval centre now submerged. Where today the main road leads straight over the cliff. You could explore ancient Dunwich, I suggested. Alfonso was not greatly interested. Our spotlights are not strong under water, he replied. The sands are moving everywhere. In the North Sea we are sailing over a desert.

The Martello tower to the south was up for sale. Alfonso ignored it. Now he was ignoring everything. He said he was preoccupied by the task of refloating. It was dangerous to refloat a submarine, it could easily get damaged. It could even break in two. It would be a hazardous manoeuvre. Not everyone could stay up safely on deck.

I nodded.

In truth submarining was a hard life, he continued. You had to suppress fear of small spaces. Fear of slicks of oil. Of having nowhere to go when you had to get out. There were no windows, nowhere to jump. Even the captain's bunk was impossibly narrow. He had not turned over in a bed for eighteen months. It was like sleeping on a plank. Death in a submarine was excruciating; life in one . . .

Slamming us from nowhere, a new wind blew his sentence to a standstill. We paused to get adjusted to the bluster.

Soon, he assured me, we would be rounding the spit where the vessel was. First we would see the conning tower—the ancient conning tower, like a funnel—then the grey upper half. Then, depending on the tide, the red lower half and, although beached, something of the glory of the great cigar.

The wind dropped as we turned the corner.

There were clumps of reeds in what also looked like a lagoon.

The captain shivered.

This is wrong, he said. This is not as it should be.

In what way?

There was not nearly so much water here before, he replied.

This really is a lagoon, I said firmly.

I know what's in your mind, he said suddenly, bitterly. It's obvious. You think there is no *Isaac Peral*. But I must tell you this is of no importance to me, none at all. What does it matter what you think? What does it matter, now or later?

I suppose not.

At least you have not seen her beached. I said you would see her glory, but in truth *el cigarre* on land is not a pretty sight.

Alfonso, I said turning to face him, I think you owe me an explanation.

Alfonso shrugged.

I do not think this, he said.

Let me guess, I said. You are going to say they have left you behind.

Yes, they have left me behind. But why are you angry? It is a difficult, terrible situation.

Having missed the seminar, I settled for watching the currents cross the golden shingle one last time.

So where are you from Alfonso? I said. What are you doing here?

I told you, it is of no importance.

We looked at the sections of North Sea water, great tarpaulins of grey and yellow. Like a compass needle, the captain turned to gaze beyond the lagoon entrance. He was facing the direction of Belgium, where a small wave rippled as at first four struts, then the periscope, then the ancient conning tower broke the surface.

Untitled

To prolong the moment of orgasm, Anna cerebrally considered the orange light filling the curtainless windows. With two fingers she circled slowly. Said the words *orange light* through two circles. *Berlin*, a circle. Slower. Applying almost no pressure, she wanted everything light. *Ja, den där er god*. Paul Klee (for she knew her modern art) took this orange to paint a landscape, calling it the colour of drum skins. Was drumskin one word, or two, drum skin? Her skin. Her ever-perspiring skin. Anna looked down, watched herself circling. Felt herself edge out of control—*den där er god*, she said out loud, *mycket fint*—as she saw her strong thighs. She caught the sole of one foot moving in the little mirror in the corner, caught its curves, the slim shape that could be held in a hand. *Ja*. Orange sky, why was it orange, because of winter, because of so many volcanoes erupting over the world? Reaching up, orange sky, window-panes, one word or two, round, slowly. *Ja, den där er god*. The sky at midnight had been barely yellow. Hours of barely yellow on more barely yellow, building to orange by morning. Vast Berlin cast under a lampshade of light. Anna looked down, shut her eyes. Anna Cederquist longing for something, coming.

The sound of the door closing passed round the walls. Paul Bernadis had ceased to believe the usual human signals and took the interrogator absenting himself for a sign men would enter and beat him.

Ten minutes passed.

Bernadis began to think. He had been brought in a van, not a car. Cars were for "interesting persons". So he might not be shot; not today. But why this cavernous room? So emptied, stripped of furnishings, files, what had been here? Was it for meetings? Conferences? He found no answers.

Weary on his feet, he let his head hang. Now morning, it had been evening when he was told they were coming for him. He had been given most of the night hours to think about them coming. He hadn't slept, hard though he'd tried. An alert, well-rested man is of no use to the interrogator; he wants someone who has lost his nerve before the interrogation even begins.

He was hungrier than ever. He had eaten with his hands tied behind his back, lost most of the soup. He wondered how long his hands had been tied. His wrists had thinned. Soon he could even slip his hands out if he wanted, should he be foolish enough.

The interrogator said he would be back in ten minutes. The man had looked ill. Unusual things were going on, as if the situation was shifting. Why was he not in front of a judge in the people's court? Why this room? He guessed: because something had happened to the room he was supposed to be in. What? Were the Russians outside the city? Surely not? The Americans? Where was he? He had arrived in pitch darkness.

Anna showered at her perspiration and towelled at it and powdered and creamed it and finally she lost interest and stretched and admired herself and pretended to practise ballet in the long mirror. After admiring her strong legs she got dressed. What luck to have been loaned an apartment. But what would she do in Berlin?

One of the lights, a white globe hung from the high ceiling, buzzed like an insect and went out. The guard—the big man, was he called Schroeder?—stepped to the interrogator's table and switched on a lamp.

Bernadis looked at the objects spilled on the table. His fiancée's effects. Effects? Belongings. A purse. The cigarette case she kept for cigarettes to give to others. You should see her at the prison on Alexanderplatz, the interrogator had said. Whatever that meant. It was six weeks since he had seen Meta. The honeymoon postponed *until the end of the war.* Did he believe there would be an end to the war? That he would see this end? Where had they said? Near Göteburg, said Meta. *Yerterborg.*

He believed nothing and he told them nothing. When he found the strength he said things like, "You have sentenced people to death for merely listening to enemy broadcasts. I don't deny I have listened to them myself." But no real information, no matter what they did or said, as he did not believe divulging information would stop anything, change anything. No deals could be trusted. He had been beaten, whipped, kicked. Since the day his hands were tied he had fallen several times on his head. At least two teeth were missing, others broken. Blood stuck the underwear to his skin.

He had been left alone with two SS guards; Meta's purse and cigarette case on the table. He longed to cross the floor to the windows. The open space began to produce an added anxiety in him. Apart from the interrogator's chair and lamp all objects and pictures, had there been any, had been removed from the room. The table had been bolted to the floor.

No doubt the *Time Out* guide was excellent, Anna speculated, but reading it depressed her. She felt every stone in Berlin had already been upturned. Every twist in its history had been documented and turned inside out and back again. Whatever else she heard—from acquaintances, newspaper articles, on television, the internet—everyone said the same. Berlin was scarred by its many histories: it was vibrant: it was developing, *becoming* itself. But Anna wanted not to be intimidated by these certainties. She wanted the very paving stones to look up and see her calves, to acknowledge that, undaunted by the weight of this history, she would be tripping along with a light step, playing, skating. At the thought of skating she looked out at the Lietzensee lake below the apartment. There were dozens of skaters on the ice. With the snow bringing down the volume of traffic, the air would be fresh, cooling. Nevertheless Anna Cederquist feared going out of the building would take away her lightness, draw her to an inevitable darkness.

With the sky paling Bernadis asked to be allowed to look out of the window. Each few days that he found himself still alive he requested some small thing like this, voicing a small need so as to remind himself he had a will. He received no reply from the guards. No one moved.

Bernadis asked again to look out of the window. The guards looked at each other.

Was this the quiet before the beating? The last time was at the Gestapo building on Prinz Albrecht Strasse. Six men had entered the room and positioned themselves in a circle—to pick up rubber truncheons, whips and clubs, which had been put in the room beforehand. He had scrambled onto a pile of books but they pulled him down and beat him until the interrogator told them to stop.

Anna made herself coffee, telling herself not to drink more the same day. More caffeine: more sweat. More sweat: more blotchy skin. She sat on the sofa leafing through the Berlin Zitty magazine. Suddenly she got it: *Zitty* is like *city*. But what will she do? She will go to the courtyards and shops of the Hackescher Höfe, reputedly the inplace for tourists. Tourists that's me, she said to the white walls and the row of CDs, the short shelf of books. That's me, she repeated to the doll on the sofa, the two bright red artificial poppies on wire.

Bernadis asked a third time. One guard went to the door and immediately he feared. When the last interrogator had stopped the beating the same questions got asked. Replying, he had stuck to his earlier, sparse statements. An hour later five other men came in and beat him again. Then one placed a chair in the middle of the room and ordered him to raise his arm and give the Hitler salute. He didn't give it. After another beating he followed the order to make the salute. "This fellow has the cheek to salute us with 'Heil Hitler'," complained one of the thugs, and for this he was laid into again.

His mind blanked. The guard might simply be talking to the guards outside. There were always guards outside.

He tried to fight down a great thirst. He pictured Meta in her smart long coat. Her smile and short brown hair. The smouldering look he thought of her as having. He thought he sensed some saliva. He swallowed, but his throat was dry, his tongue like a dead leaf.

The guard came back in, closed the door, looked up at the light that no longer worked. His cheeks were rosy now. He had probably been out of the building. Looking down slowly, theatrically, he made it seem he was noticing Bernadis for the first time.

Well, he said, well. Somebody wants to look out of the window. This window? he gestured. That window?

Any window, Bernadis said in a cracked voice.

Now it's any window.

His boots squeaking on the parquet floor, he walked slowly up to a window.

It's only the first floor, said the big man.

There. A window. Don't do any damage.

As Paul moved they moved with him. Starting too eagerly, he fell. With his hands tied, his head cracked into the wood boards. Immediately the door opened. Schroeder? called a guard. It's nothing, said the guard who had been outside, who was not Schroeder. The heavy door thudded shut on the three men, the sound slamming through Bernadis on the floor. Still conscious, he lay next to a boot which was wet from somewhere, perhaps rain, even snow. He refused to turn his head, waiting for the incident to be somehow used against him.

It's nothing, said rosy cheeks sarcastically. A stupid fall. A fall without grace. No grace, no patience. Hurry, hurry is not always the best policy. But there's no time to learn that now. Is there, Schroeder? In fact there's no time to learn *anything*.

Schroeder sighed, troubled; out of tune with the more talk-ative guard. Bernadis failed to decipher the oblique comments, the sigh, but sensed panic in the air. He put one ear flush to the shining floor to see how the wood felt. It was cold, icy. He glanced quickly at his guards. Rosy cheeks. At the big man, whose dark hair brushed up in straight lines.

Get up, said Schroeder.

His wrists in agony, Bernadis rolled over. He rocked from side to side until he managed to sit. Pain flared from one cheekbone. Astonishingly, Schroeder stepped forward and helped him to stand. The gesture troubled him. They walked. The pain vanished. Before Bernadis got to the window, now of enormous importance, the pristine look of the glass struck him as a marvel. So pure that he wondered if there really was glass; if there wasn't air between the thick cross-pieces and the bars.

He was thrust right up to the panes. By chance there was a proper view, onto the street. It had been snowing. There were tyre marks in the snow, no one was about. Bernadis, who had turned guessing the time into a task, a contact with something beyond his immediate situation, put it at between six-thirty and seven. Looking hurriedly, furtively for information, clues to something, he caught the faint reflection of the building in the windows of the building opposite. He saw mirrored the great eagle over the doorway. Flanking the eagle were two great shoulders of stone, crude and curving. So he was inside the military court building. This was not normal. It was for traitors. For deserters, Nazis themselves in the resistance.

Nonetheless the sight of outside braced him. He even remem-bered something Meta had said: *if only Napoleon had had tanks*. He wanted to see her below. He wanted to be whole, with Meta as they were.

An ice-hockey pitch had been cleared on the frozen lake. Looking down on the players, Anna felt her skin cool as she watched young teenagers fall on snow piled on the sidelines. But she hesitated from going out and returned to the sofa, the Zitty magazine and her guide. She was determined to have a good time, was that a contradiction in terms? Should she leave with a resolute plan or be ready to change with the circumstances? What if a man tried to pick her up? That would depend on the person. If a woman? But she could, as a matter of prior decision, avoid these things in advance. She could leave the apartment with some unswerving aim, and so fulfil herself. But where to? The dilemma with the Hackescher Höfe was that the buildings used to be Jewish; there would be no escaping the presence of Jews. Now that they had gone, in the way they had gone, would they not always be present in Berlin? Especially at such a place. Anna feared the Höfe would embroil her in a terrible story of deportations, shootings, men humiliated, women screaming. Children beside trains in bravely smart clothes, separated from their parents. She suddenly thought of her grandparents, who had been taken away by the Nazis.

Bernadis stared at the roofs and the sky. If Helen of Troy had launched and sunk a thousand ships, Meta's smile would have raised them back out of the water. Everyone remarked on her smile. Had she lost it now? It would come back, would it not? When Meta smiled for him Paul had gone with her on the tram to a fine address to which she had the key. He lost his tongue when she undressed, having expected her to be beautiful but not so beautiful, to be strong but not so strong. You're beautiful, he managed to get out at last. She told him to hurry taking his socks off. How many lovers had she had? he asked, so stupidly asked. One, she said simply. Thomas Steinhofer. Oh, Thomas Steinhofer. Who is he? My life thread, she said secretively, my passport.

This man is a mess, said the rosy-cheeked guard. He needs a bucket of water thrown over him.

Not on this fine floor, said the other. Not here.

But he stinks. Schroeder, I'm outside if you need me.

You mean you—No I don't, Meta said: he will do anything for me, but I won't for him. Paul wondered if this Thomas Steinhofer had anything to do with the fine address to which she had the key, but said nothing. He had been clumsy enough in asking his asinine question. Instead he reached out to touch one of her ears, she had the most perfect ears. You want a virgin, Meta had gone on talking as they lay down: what use would that be to you? The exchange had made his blood surge. Hoping to end the subject, he bid her to turn over and kissed the fine hairs on her neck. I don't want a virgin, she had said into the pillow. Sh, Bernadis had said. Sh, Meta.

That too was a mistake. Later she corrected him: Paul, when you told me to stop talking I stopped talking then but make no mistake I won't generally. They had just candles: she looked so brown in the candlelight. With me, Paul Bernadis, she said sat on his lap, you'll get the rugged and the tender. But you'll know what you've got. It was these forthright words, in statements that tumbled out one after another, that time and again had made him sit up. Slow to respond, he felt he needed to run to catch up with her. This feeling had never left him, not since he asked his stupid questions and she fired back without fear.

He still pictured her, at the fine address in the candlelight. They made love, telling each other not to be loud, whispering this so many times they began laughing, then telling each other not to laugh so loud, then trying to laugh in whispers, making everything quite impossible, then bursting and roaring, completely losing control.

Time, said Schroeder suddenly.

Time? said Bernadis.

You can't stay at the window. It looks bad.

The answers she gave were her answers, not the answers he would like to have heard. The more he understood this, the more love he felt. He loved Meta, Meta rugged and tender, he trusted her.

Is bad, Schroeder was saying. It is not good that you think. It helps nothing, no one. To think is to put yourself in danger.

Put myself in danger? thought Bernadis: what an absurd remark to hear in his situation.

Come on, said Schroeder glancing back at the door, we've been here long enough.

Bernadis focused all his thinking on one point: I want to stay at the window; I will stay at the window.

As if a wind had blown, the door clicked gently open but immediately shut. There was no voice, no footsteps. No one had entered.

Schroeder brushed back his hair with his hand.

The sky is orange, said Bernadis.

Schroeder sighed, moved his weight onto the other foot.

Orange? It's the time of year.

Time of year? said Bernadis. You mean winter?

What did you think I meant?

I hadn't been aware of it—before, said Bernadis. Perhaps, I was thinking, it's the building opposite. It's orange too.

Schroeder pushed his chin almost onto the window pane, revealing a cut on his neck he must have made shaving, and quickly glanced both ways.

Orange bricks, remarked Bernadis.

It's a school, said Schroeder. Look over the entrance. *Mädchen-Schule*, it says, number 22. *Knaben-Schule*, 21.

A school, Bernadis repeated. It will start soon.

This met a laugh. The door opened. The rosy-cheeked, wet-booted guard indicated he would change places with Schroeder, who left the room.

The guard smelled of freshly smoked cigarette.

You see the light overhead? he said.

Bernadis did not look up.

I'm aware of it, he said.

Stand under it.

Anna Cederquist pulled herself together and left the building wrapped in gloves, woollen hat and bright blue scarf. The temperature had become unbudging at below zero. Wooden sleds and red and grey toboggans launched themselves down the snow-packed banks of the lake; the heaviest, bearing happy fathers, went gliding far across its icy plateau. A fast-flitting red squirrel shook down powdery snow from a tree. It's a winter wonderland, said Anna to herself as she ducked playfully at snowballs which did not get thrown.

Heading for the underground station of Sophie Charlotte Platz, she fell in behind a miniature snowplough which was clearing a path on the pavement. First absorbed trying to read black stencilling on the orange cab, she then followed the vehicle like a child, turning this corner and that, until she unwittingly entered a street, dark with stone, which dispatched a dread chill, a cloak of cold on her shoulders. It's the delirium the doctor warned of, she told herself half-heartedly, the extreme manifestation of *hyperhidrosis*. Or it's an eclipse. She half-expected there to be a body in the snow; for someone to loom up behind her. Then she saw, registered with her eyes: a building, huge and heavy with granite. Dark, abandoned-looking. Once a bank, offices, a ministry? Its stone neither brown nor grey, the building radiated an aura of cold—which not only settled on Anna but travelled up and down her in waves, would not let her be. What was this place?

Looking up, Anna saw flowers hewn in the stone, minimal decorations which she next saw were not properly flowers. Feeling chilled—assailed—she hurried past double metal doors etched with blue rust, hurried to overtake the snowplough, almost stumbling beside it in the banks of snow. The driver smiled at her in her hat and scarf. He stopped. For you, he said gallantly, his arms spread. Anna didn't get it. For her? The snow, the plough? *For you*? What kind of German was that?

She walked quickly back a few steps to escape the situation. But to escape what? The driver of a snowplough? She could have smiled back at him and walked on in front. Too late. Feeling ridiculous standing behind the now idling vehicle, not wishing a further exchange with the driver, she tramped resolutely back the way she had come. When she heard the plough continue she shuddered from the cold; the dark presence returned. She felt under a belljar of darkness. Fearing this might somehow cast a shadow across her day, Anna decided she would nonetheless have to try to exorcise it, go back to the building, look again.

Approaching it for the second time, from its other end, she realized one reason the building emanated darkness was that almost no snow had collected on it, not even on the stubby steep roof above. Below the roof she thought she saw two fish; but the images in the stonework, like the flowers which weren't flowers, or the colours which weren't nameable colours, were again nothing proper, nothing recognisable. The scales were like reptile scales but were joined to no figures, no heads. Then she saw the eagle, then the chiselled capitals disappearing into the stone, REICHS MILITAER GERICHT.

The guard told Bernadis the interrogator would return in an hour. Bernadis knew not to trust this information. He tussled with ways he could find out what was going on. Where was the interrogator? What was wrong with him? This could not be asked outright, that was inconceivable. He tried formulations on himself.

The investigator has been gone a long time.

Not his business.

The investigator did not look well.

Equally, not his business.

These were indeed questions, too thinly veiled. What if he offered something?

My fiancée's name is Meta, Meta Stenevi.

This sounded like information, though it would be information already known. But the subject matter could lead to unforeseeable difficulties. The guard might say something terrible; say what they might have done to her. No, he needed a much cleverer line. At best, something where every word implied his own inferiority. An entirely innocuous remark, not threatening or provoking.

The sky is orange. He was able to say that to Schroeder. But to the guard who was not Schroeder?

So, said the guard speaking first, you are not asking to look out of the window again. Though there is much to see. There are big clouds in the sky.

Bernadis tried to clear his throat. He was certain something was shaking up the situation. As if an earthquake was reaching towards them from beneath their feet. For a guard did not talk this way. Schroeder, certainly, had gone too far; had *talked to him*. No, no investigator would be returning to this room this day.

I just said, the guard repeated, you have no more interest in the window.

I already saw out of the window, said Bernadis.

So you did. And what did you see?

A school. The sky you just referred to. It has been snowing.

So you talked to—

Schr . . . He told me that was a school.

Why?

I don't know.

He just—told you?

The door burst open.

Enveloped still by the dark from the building, bearing it like a hood, Anna boarded the underground. The carriage was small, with yellow light and fake-veneered caramel panels. Benches ran longways, alongside the windows. Sensing a need to be on her guard, Anna made an effort to shake off the hood and sat straight and alert. A man with matted hair and tattoos and a pitbull went through the carriage wanting money and started a snarling argument with a man with an accordion on his lap. A man with a guitar and a styrofoam cup sang "Till there was you" in a thin, whining voice and was given nothing. A woman with a bruised face and crutches and feet wrapped in silver foil wanted money and stabbed her crutches at people's feet before going motionless, stiller than a fish, with her cheek pressed against the panels at one end of the carriage. Perturbed and still undecided about whether to go to the Hackescher Höfe, Anna broke her journey at Savignyplatz. Under the arches of the station she entered a café and without enjoyment drank a *café cortado*, a drink she had discovered the previous summer in Spain.

She sat in the café hoping to rid herself of the recollection of the man with the dog and the woman with her feet wrapped in foil. The chill of the street with the building returned to her shoulders. If only she had not followed the snowplough she would have kept her lightness, the pavement would have looked up and seen her tripping along. But, as she feared, she had been drawn to the dark things and now she had seen them and there was no going back.

The coffee began to disgust her; the heavy passage of another train overhead reverberated through her being. Even the weather, which she had delighted in that morning, began to annoy her. More walking would turn her wet boots even wetter. She was supposed to *rotate her shoes*, she had read at the doctor's in a list of measures against the evils of sweating. Socks and shoes, moods, hormones, drugs, caffeine and alcohol, hyperhidrosis, hyperthyroidism, *air your feet, rotate your shoes*. She thought about this list one last time, determined never to worry herself again about the stupidly interminable matter of sweat. She looked at herself in the mirror beside the coffee machines, then looked away. She turned in on herself.

Anna Cederquist, 23, on holiday in Berlin, stopped caring.

There was a great commotion in the corridor.

Quick, called Schroeder. We're going. The whole of 4D3. Everyone.

I thought so, said the other guard. You see to him.

What about him?

Leave him.

Leave him?

What Schroeder said next was inaudible as somewhere, down the stairs, maybe in a courtyard, the street, doors to vehicles could be heard slamming, orders shouted, engines turned and revved.

That's right, Schroeder. Padlock him to the window. Put this chain around his wrists, round those cords. He likes the window. He will have a front seat.

Front seat to what? said Bernadis to Schroeder as he hurriedly checked the lock and the key. Suddenly the big man smelled of urine.

You may be lucky, said rosy cheeks from the doorway. Though I doubt it. I'm going. Schroeder, you lock the room.

Wait. Riedel. There's nowhere to put a chain by the window.

Stop panicking and do your job.

There is nowhere, insisted Schroeder.

Well that's too bad, just too bad. Use the table. Let him sniff his woman's things. And hurry. I'll be down in the yard.

Take me with you, whispered Bernadis.

That's impossible, said Schroeder crouched beside him.

I have a fiancée.

I know.

I think she's pregnant. I've heard.

Pregnant? You tell me she's pregnant? What am I supposed to do? Pregnant?

She may be. This is going to be bombed, isn't it?

Maybe not. Not now. Not by daylight. There'll be nothing for hours.

You think.

Yes, we think, said Schroeder. We think we know.

Where are you going?

I'm not sure. I can't say.

Where is my fiancée?

You heard: in the prison on Alexanderplatz. But she may be moved, who can say.

You must know.

How should I know?

Rottenführer Schroeder! Kommen Sie!

I have finished. I will lock the door.

Schroeder, don't chain me to the table, open the lock. I can't get out through these windows. My hands are tied. Just lock me in the room, it's enough.

All right.

Yes.

Goodbye.

Good—bye.

Deliberately taking the wettest, snowiest streets, Anna came to a bookshop. She found a section on German history and looked for the *Reichs Militär Gericht*, the regime's military court. She looked in every book and found not a single mention of it. She moved on to a bigger shop, with escalators and islands of tables and walls of shelves so long they almost disappeared from view. She came across the very photographs of children she had feared finding. A Hungarian girl aged about twelve awaiting deportation stared hard into the camera, her coat unbuttoned. The girl's eyebrows were hardened into a look of accusation which went deeper than accusation. The look said she knew what was being done to her, done to her terrified brother beside her, as they stood both in the same coats, the same cheap wool collars. His coat buttoned, hers undone, her breasts just beginning. Anna held the book weakly, helplessly at her side, and stared blearily at the shelves. She heaved a sigh, then held the picture again squarely before her. The girl's unbuttoned coat told a plain tale: she was utterly indifferent to whether it was buttoned; such a question was entirely without purpose. Suddenly Anna felt she and the girl were looking at each other. The hard look, the unbuttoned coat: Anna knew the sight of this girl looking straight into the camera would not leave her.

She put the book down.

So it was, she thought. It was impossible, and it was.

What about her own grandparents, who had been taken away as dissenters?

Anna discovered there was a memorial centre for the German resistance, the *Gedenkstätte Deutscher Widerstand*, with papers and photographs and information. She consulted her map and set out immediately.

Once the tramp of feet had ceased, the sound of the vehicles vanished, and for a long time there had been no more vehicles, no sounds, Bernadis persuaded himself that Meta was with him and resolved not to panic. He told her he would proceed systematically. First he would find a way to free his hands. Next he would find a way to leave the room. Although it was highly dangerous to leave the room it was highly dangerous to stay, besides which he needed food, water.

By turning one wrist around so it lay flush with the other, he was able to free his hands. Locked or unlocked, the padlock would not have kept him bound to the table. Not a hair was left on his wrists. He touched his face. There were rough, painful places. He wanted water. He went to the window. He tried to see his face in it and couldn't. Footprints and tyre tracks were everywhere.

The snow outside made him aware of the cold. I can see quite a way down the street, Meta, both ways. There is no one there.

Its only grace the cluster of buildings soaring skywards in their new grey glass and steel, Potsdamer Platz was a windswept wasteland within the larger windswept wasteland, the still-empty heart of Berlin. Anna had read that Sony and Daimler-Chrysler had here created the new cathedrals of their time. There were no signs to the *Gedenkstätte*, no street signs, she had no sense of direction at all. She headed for the huge dome of the Sony Center hoping to orient herself, and came to a shopping mall which seemed to lie across the street on her map. Shopping malls are the museums of the future, Andy Warhol had said. A mall is a mall, Anna found herself thinking. Is *the* mall. At Potsdamer Platz, like anywhere, the shops were the shops which always were the shops; commerce had yet to devise a strategy for concealing this fact. She had walked through the entire centre, she realized, *as if it was not there*. The Sony dome itself was extraordinarily futuristic, and would be for a while, she guessed, but was a place which would surely one day be bombed, a cast-iron certainty, it was crying out to be bombed one way or another. Lost thinking these things, she had walked down a street with no name which led to a wire fence which cordoned off a vast hole in the ground. She went back and took another street with no name. Cold winds blew about the tall buildings. She wrapped up tighter.

Anna Cederquist, all this time feeling an immeasurable weight, bearing an ache, the ache passed to her by the girl in the picture, that coat forever open.

She could remember the buttons, could see there had been no buttons missing.

Bernadis tried the door. It was locked, heavy, oak, impenetrable, unopenable. He knew little about bombs, although he understood the main blasts generally occurred on the lower floors, blowing out the windows and doors. The various woods of the furniture and floors, he had been told, could be crucial in softening or hardening the effect of a blast. But this knowledge was vague and of no use. All he knew, he told himself, was that until he was dead, he was alive. He stayed at the window and struggled to keep his mind active. He wanted to count the tiles on the steep roof of the school, but the snow thwarted him. He wanted to determine the exact direction he was facing, but the sun did not appear. No shadows, no clock. Without a clock even the sun would be useless. He realised a chain hung across a door of the school; the windows were shut and boarded from inside.

Flushed from the cold, Anna walked on. Away from the dome she came to a crossroads with traffic lights in the middle of desolate roads and sickly pine trees which stood shambolically, in a stupid mess, at one corner. Following the dual carriageway beside the pines, she eventually stood before a concert hall which her map said was the home of the Berlin Philharmonic. Next she came to a museum for musical instruments. She was surrounded by modern buildings, no people, no signs. A feeling of what could be delirium returned. Was it her or where she was? Again she tried orienting herself. That must be the Tiergarten park. There's a sign to the zoo, but the zoo must be miles away. That could be the Neue Nationalgalerie. Closed.

It's still light, he registered, still quiet. He must have slept. Bernadis spent minutes imbibing the quiet. He breathed deliberately, slowly. So quiet. No matter, Meta, the silence isn't hurting. Now that I'm getting used to it, I hear birds nearby. They have reappeared, daring to sing. I can't see any, but I think they're those birds that live in the brown creepers that spill and trail all the way down the buildings in this city. I don't know what those creepers are called. But you know which trees and birds they are, you do, you're just teasing me not telling. So don't speak, you don't have to speak. I won't speak either, but I'm thinking, making decisions. I would speak were my throat not so dry. I have decided to give myself one night in which to recoup. I may have a better chance if I wait. In the meantime I will break a window with my elbow, or a fist; I have to plan this well. I can take snow from the sill and drink from it, although very little has settled on there. I mustn't make too big a hole in the pane because of the cold. It's cold already, but only a little bit cold. Then I should keep away from the windows in case there's a bombardment. Under the table perhaps.

Anna was exhausted by the time she found the *Gedenkstätte*, a quiet building with a quietly imposing courtyard laid with a fine mosaic of tiny, flat grey stones. The two floors of exhibits occupied a vast area, with almost every text on the boards in German, a language which constantly tired her and she did not feel comfortable with. The galleries of photographs and boards on the walls and documents and drawers of information went on and on. Moving quickly for the most part, stopping occasionally, she walked all the galleries. In the vast series of rooms she saw just three other visitors.

At the information desk she asked about the military court building and was directed to a section about justice. She read the boards. Apparently a semblance of justice had been important to the regime, as it was thought this lent it authenticity and legitimacy, hence shoring up public support. But the need to follow proper procedures had waned over time. Black and white photographs showed men in suits standing before the crowded People's Court, some arguing eloquently and making brave stands, others awaiting sentencing in silence. Accounts of the proceedings were splashed all over newspapers, their paper now yellowed, the finicky but orderly script (what did they call that?) hard to read. Anna stayed mostly with the photographs, taking care not to look at any with children, and was struck by the innocuousness of the head-and-shoulders photos of those on trial. They looked indifferent, even pleasant, everything but criminal. The papers denounced those who had resisted as traitors, as tiny cliques of conspirators. The reports ended with the sentences handed down, but other documents went on to tell how the accused were hung, shot, given lethal injections or deported to camps—shown like pocks on a map, in a terrible rash all across Germany—where they were often shot, gassed or became part of the general so-called extermination through labour. The accounts and the photographs went on and on. One man was photographed having perished in an aerial attack which would otherwise have liberated him. Another had been made to join a bomb disposal squad, another was shown lying across the electric fence of a concentration camp. Then there were pictures of children.

Anna went outside.

I hear the birds as a message: if they can recover and sing then surely we can as well. We'll speak brightly, look decent again. See me now: I look like a gorilla. An apt likeness—given I've decided to give my dry throat a rest—because gorillas can't speak (I've heard, because they don't have our windpipes, our something). Beasts, they don't share our good fortune in speaking. And what fortune that is. To think I can say things to you—and what a magic effect they have. When you say you will love me once the war is over (that's what you said Meta), what an effect that has. But even just to say to you, I will meet you on the corner at seven, and see that this works, is a miracle. You look at the clock—look at the clock and take down your long coat and there we are, on the corner at seven. Two gorillas could not manage this meeting. Even if one went to the corner at seven, Meta, it would be a gorilla in a thousand, and the other would not be there but somewhere else, not even at another corner; and there are so many corners.

You said you want us to go to Mexico once the war is over, once the Atlantic is safe again. We'll go, to a place by the sea. We'll sit next to trees with soft barks and leaves big as tablecloths and watch pelicans dive in the water. Our children will run in mad circles around us. How the sun will set. How good we'll feel just being alive. We'll come back penniless but happy, back to our house by the forest, by a lake, by a field. There is so much we have yet to decide, Meta, so many forks in the road to take together. I will make a new start, with hard but honest toil—as a fisherman, farmer, forester. You will go back to your studies. At home together, surrounded by our children, we'll argue the small things. You want a bird house: I think a bird table. You will want the door painted red: I will say blue. Darling

Meta, this is what we will talk about after the end of the war. Your purse is on the table, did you see? It doesn't feel as if there's anything in it, look, there isn't. I'll shut the clasp again. Thank you for bringing it, I may use it when I break through the glass. I'll get you another, with a zip fastener. All our children will have purses with zip fasteners. Malin, and Lotta, and Kennet and Freja, all those wonderful names.

The birds are getting louder. When I break the glass they'll be three times as loud, I'll be the first medical case of going deaf from bird song. I shall break the glass soon, take some snow. Once I have water, Meta, I can clean myself, or you can clean me if you are up to it. Water, so miraculous: the way it flows down and over, taking the dirt with it and leaving things whole; the fact we can drink it, that it keeps us alive. What an invention water would be if someone discovered it. No one would believe the inventor. Go away, they would say, you're crazy. That's what they say to inventors. *What*, they'll say, not only can we drink it, we can throw ourselves *into* it? Get out, they'll say, go, take your water, your taps and bottles and paddles and canoe, your fishing net and kettle and soap! We can turn it to ice, the inventor will say at the door, keep food fresh. Out in the street he goes. He chucks away his water and immediately it turns to ice, to snow. Children play with it. Our children will play with it. There must be a lot of that in Sweden, Meta, children playing with snow, skating, whatever else you can do in Yerterborg. At our summer house outside the city. Wherever, it doesn't matter where. Almost everywhere in the world there is water.

Now I'll sleep. Wake up to you and a new sky, new clouds. Feel a fresh shirt on my skin, be pleased at the firmness of the buttons. But first to sleep. What a pleasure it will be when we sleep. With a pillow that fits, eyes closed; our minds winding down, our problems dissolving away for the night. When you say the way we pleasure each other is a god, darling Meta, pleasuring us and binding us, I say sleep too is a god. When we lie and sleep we enter a new life, where everything changes, which our inventor never could dream of. Such pleasure. It feels so good, Meta, Meta so good.

So she had found no mention of the military court. No book with it listed in its index. Clearly there were more terrible places, courts, prisons, execution yards.

Anna hung about in the courtyard laid with the fine mosaic of stones, undecided what to do next.

Soldiers came and went, for the *Gedenkstätte* was also part of the headquarters of the army of today.

She looked at the sky and wondered if it would snow again that day.

Eventually Anna Cederquist walked out of the courtyard and turned down the street, in the direction of the Tiergarten and the pine trees. She allowed herself to leave by telling herself she would be coming again.

Taiga

Down the concrete tunnel in the hospital catacomb Ms Dorn surged beside me. Scarf surging, surging handbag over surging shoulder. *Ship's figurehead, Greta Garbo, Queen Christina.* Queen Dorn surging, scarf (autumn colours) tied sweetly but smartly, one gold square facing forwards. It was an effort to keep up. It's my first real walk in a week Ms Dorn. Good, she said looking ahead. Good? I queried. Good to have something to work on—so she said looking on ahead, expecting great deeds; but deeds well in the distance, not in the tunnel with me.

The moments of desire, Ms Dorn, that appeared in that time and will open out over years, that you will never know.

At the end of the tunnel men in blue overalls hosed down a concrete floor. Aura of kitchens, giant grey saucepans, ribbed sides of cow. Arctic temperature, puddles on concrete. Are such the sites of true romance?

With Ms Dorn bearing down the overalled men pointed the nozzles aside at some drains. Ahead and brightly lit, a ramp opened to the outer world, to bright blankets of teeming snowflakes. Ms Dorn would clearly go straight on, up the ramp. To her bus, her car, her shopping, her man?

She turned full-frontally.

To get to the library you go down those stairs.

That dirty green staircase?
Down there. Goodbye.
Goodbye.
I love you, Ms Dorn.

Ms Dorn, wait, what were you thinking as we were walking along? I have a savings account. I know people. I can get together ten thousand pounds. Tell me what you were thinking and I will give you ten thousand pounds.

You can't leave the hospital.

By taxi I can. We can get this taxi here. Go to my place, I'll get some street clothes, we'll go straight from there to the bank.

OK. Let's go.

You believe me?

You seem honest. Or should I close my eyes until I see the money? That's not a bad idea. Stay in the taxi while I get my clothes.

That was quick.

I'm quick. These clothes will do. There's the bank already. How do you want the money?

Ah, fifty-pound notes will be quite all right.

They're counting them by hand.

So I see. Thank you.

So what were you thinking, as we were walking?

I was thinking, there's no way I'm going to get involved with him.

That's heartening, almost. You were thinking about me.

I think that about everyone on the ward.

Not everyone. Not Malcolm—

I don't discuss other patients. And when I say I think that, I don't need to think about it, I know so. But we're getting outside our brief. Unless you have another ten thousand, but you don't.

So what else were you thinking?

Otherwise I was thinking about broccoli. How much to buy, whether to buy a lot or a little, enough for one meal or two.

Wh—

Now I have ten thousand pounds, I have decided to buy a lot. I may even get a pound of leeks. Goodbye again. I will make my own way home. If you want the library, try reception once you get back. Or you could start again at the lifts.

Then down those stairs?
Down there. Goodbye.

Swaggering back from his consultation, Malcolm stepped up to the panorama window looking over the west of the city. I followed, holding onto a table, a bed, the window-catch.

The sun shone on white roofs and open spaces.

Malcolm of the thick wavy grey hair, big fruity face, poked my arm, wheezed indecipherable words. Beautiful! he scrawled on his pad. He put his thumbs up. *Snow!*

He held up successive handfuls of fingers. Seventeenth floor. Big, he wheezed with his arms wide, meaning the window.

It was big. We woke to the sun in the bottom left, looked for it later overhead; slept as it set bottom right.

The sight excited him to a wheezing fit. His wife said he had smoked for fifty-seven years. Fifty cigarettes times fifty-seven times three hundred and sixty five. He could have bought a small house.

Malcolm, owner of no house, walked off to check in the mirror. In place of a house he had a new Persil-white bow tie arrangement, a blue microphone with a millefleur design on his throat. It was pretty, circus pretty.

Smart, he said stepping back from the mirror. Smarter than the old plastic. Bakelite, they used to call that. Here GOES, he said as he switched his new device on.

That hospital shirt looks terrible, said Ms Dorn. Surely you're not going to keep wearing that.

Won't believe this, Malcolm had put on his pad.

When I was young, it said. I turned to the next sheet.

I was German. I was Gross, not Cross.

Not all, he scribbled.

He switched on his device.

I MARRied a Tunisian. I was crazy about her. *Ich war in sie schockverliebt.* That's the same but it's German.

You're trying to be funny.

No, no. Those were the days. Wife doesn't know.

Which wife?

Stupid, he said poking my arm. Wife now of course. I have photographs. *Photographs*, he wheezed triumphantly.

Ms Dorn appeared.

You're to go to Dr Allen, she said looking towards me.

It's good, said Malcolm clicking on the switch by his chest.

You're to use it sparingly at first, said Ms Dorn.

You don't want me. Want me talking so much.

Switch it off now.

The diagnosis is no longer Menière's disease? Should I say disease or condition?

I was trying to impress Ms Dorn with my questions at the consultation. *Ich war in sie schockverliebt.*

It's your fifth day, said tall Dr Allen. Had it been Menière's you would have recovered your balance by now. Don't worry, he said putting a hand on my shoulder, you *will* recover. Ms Dorn stood aside. She had dimples when she smiled. Her lips were large, her eyes large. Beautiful lips. My gaze never reached her hair. Her arms were by her side. When Ms Dorn looked straight at me I felt no distance between us.

The big window by night. The docks a string of tawny lights in the distance. Twinkling orange blips: containers moving. Down below was the bending, now empty street that always caught my eye.

I practised walking in the corridor. Suddenly Dr Allen appeared, looking for Ms Dorn.

I knew better than he did: her shift had finished hours ago.

I can't bring the photos in here of course, said Malcolm. Do you know where I've hidden them? Inside the mantelpiece.

You're crazy. How do you put photos in a mantelpiece?

Oh yes, yes, said Malcolm windmilling his arms. I even went to Tunisia. I found her. We got married. She was *drenched* in jewellery. Great. Straight into the honeymoon, on an island. An island on an island.

What do you mean?

Djerba is like an island.

I closed my eyes and the room stopped spinning. Tunisia, Tunisia. I set myself the task of finding the atlas I knew had to be in the hospital building.

I like this shirt. It's comfortable.

Feinting back and forward like a boxer, senile boxer, Malcolm poked me on the arm to hoarsely tell more about this woman he had loved. To indicate a woman he made wavy lines in the air. What woman could that be? Not Marilyn Monroe, not Madonna. The curves were too slight and there were far too many.

I turned to the bending street. Three young people in long coats were making slow headway. The perspective and the distance made them look slow.

I expect everyone to call me Ms Dorn. Sister comes originally from convents and the church. This is a hospital. I want to be called Ms, not sister. Ms Dorn.

What's that? asked Malcolm pointing to *A Plea For Eros* by Siri Hustvedt at my bedside.

I had it with me when I was taken in. Essays. Thoughts.

Thoughts, said Malcolm adjusting his new neck-piece, thoughts! Sex, you mean. When you fell and they brought you in here you could have been carrying *Playboy*. Caught with your PANTS down. Damn machine.

He tugged at the bow tie round his neck. He poked again. I was a playboy once, he said. I played with *sharks*. I was once face to face with a shark.

He demonstrated how close. He mimed the shark's part, did a pointed nose and a frozen snarl (it backed down).

Grinning, poking, he told more tales. About a Canadian bear (wrestled to the ground). A Nile crocodile (wrestled). A Turk whom he yanked towards him across a wall, whose face he pushed down into some barbed wire.

It's not the liquid that drips down that you see, said Ms Dorn adjusting the drip with one hand, it's the air going upwards.

Surely it's the water coming down.

I just told you, it is the air. That is not water either.

Some days it goes faster than others. Can I adjust it myself? *I already do.*

I'll do that.

When the sun rose on the left I lay in bed. Sister Sarah brought in breakfast.

Did you sleep well?

I didn't. Mr Cross took a shower in the night. I heard him dry himself with a hundred paper towels.

There's not many can do that here, she said taking my pulse.

Malcolm came in. It's good, he said hoarsely.

Mr Cross says he knows about an island on an island, I said to her.

Hm, she said. I'm counting. That's OK, you still have a pulse.

An island on an island, said Malcolm.

That's silly, there can't be an island on an island.

But there is, he said throatily.

That's like saying there's a lake on a lake.

Djerba is practically an island. It has sea like a big lake and an island in it.

I adjusted the drip. 500 ml were supposed to drip for four hours.

Malcolm's wife sat with him at the table.

You should eat more now you can eat again. Spread more on your bread.

Malcolm ate on.

Put it on thicker.

Malcolm ate on.

Take more slices, you've paid for it.

Ate on.

Put more cheese on. Before you take one more bite.

Shut it, Malcolm said.

I walked to the lift with the drip on its trundling stand. Away from the known world of the ward but still within protective hospital walls. I sat waiting to see Mrs Harder for the hearing tests. The reports were in my lap. One page was signed Dorn. Was in Ms Dorn's handwriting. Bold, clear, firm. At the question 'What state was the patient in when admitted?' she had marked a big blue cross at the option: *confused*.

Malcolm's wife showed us her calendar (a present for her sister) with lighthouses from all over the world. Isn't that *beautiful*? In *Ice*land. Do they have ships there Malcolm, I thought all that fishing had stopped (The cod war stopped, growled Malcolm, we stopped it with warships). And you know Maria, Malcolm (What Maria?), she *has* got that part in that soap, but you can look where you like you won't find her name in the credits. They bought *all* the TV magazines and she wasn't in one (Who's *they*?). Such a shame. Now have you eaten today? Have you had meat?

I saw Dr Allen go into the linen room. He's the tallest doctor in the place. The tallest of the tall. Ms Dorn followed him and the door closed.

I'm Mrs Harder. I'm going to test your hearing. We will see each other a few times.

Mrs Harder had a keen look, blue smock, white arms, forty-something. She gave me a beeper to press the moment I heard a sound in my ear. Our arms touched. *Good skin.*

Like a photographer waiting for the right weather, I waited to hear someone use her first name. But everyone called her Ms Dorn.

Until Dr Allen said: Mary. Mary, can you help me with this chair. Mary.

What am I to do with this name? Plain name.

I love you, Mary.

Sounds unconvincing, one name too many. Ms Dorn wants to be distant, she says. But she always stands close. Open, arms at her side. This is her framework: distance, closeness.

I turned from the window.

You're very taken by bossy Ms Dorn, said Malcolm. She doesn't wear a ring.

Doesn't wear a ring?

What do you think Malcolm, does everyone fall for the nurses in hospitals?

Malcolm shrugged. Evidently he didn't.

You know the schoolgirl in the room down the end? Teresa? Had her tonsils out?

Is she still at school?

I'll ask if she feels anything for the male nurses.

My wife in Tunisia. Ich war in sie schockverliebt.

I'll ask Teresa. She helped me walk to the coffee machine once. I might even report back.

But not when my wife's here.

On my way to the library to find an atlas to see how there was an island on an island there was Ms Dorn in the lift with her arms by her sides. I wanted to marry her and live with her, or live near her, seeing her occasionally but regularly, make love with her, once a week I would settle for, once a *month*—after a first frantic six weeks—her lips are like no other lips, full and promising love, I am on my way to the library Ms Dorn, I have made it my mission (I am trying to impress her, as a person with missions, who achieves difficult things) to find an atlas in this hospital. The library closes soon so you'll need to hurry, said Ms Dorn. In fact it may not even be open today. That won't stop me, I said over-reaching myself, I will go on until I find an atlas. Then good luck, said Ms Dorn tying her scarf. It's down this tunnel. I will show you the way.

I told Teresa Malcolm is going to have a pedicure.

She grinned.

Here you can get haircuts, shaves and a pedicure, I said. He's had shaves already. He won't let them touch his hair though.

He has a permanent wave.

He does?

Teresa nodded and grinned again. She never grins when her boyfriend visits. She lets her head sink into his shoulder, and when it comes out of there she is sad, dead from something.

How are things going with him? I asked.

OK.

Teresa's OK was a sad, dead OK.

Is he studying architecture like you?

I said I *might* study architecture.

But you do drawings.

Not in here.

Two things keep happening. I keep going to the big window. Ms Dorn keeps directing me to the library, turning me away from her to that dingy green staircase.

Are you all right?

It's night.

She always strides off to the light, leaving me with the staircase and the hoses splashing again.

When I get out of here I will practise wrapping a scarf like Ms Dorn wears hers. So smartly, sweetly.

Are you all right?

Oscar? Nurse Oscar?

Sister Sarah. OK?

I'm OK.

My father had Menère's, said Mrs Harder. The attacks stopped—

It seems I don't have Menière's, Mrs Harder.

Press this when you hear a sound in your left ear. If you hear it in your right, don't press, tell me.

Is this a carry-over of my feelings towards Ms Dorn? Mrs Harder, if you too had read A Plea For Eros *and you agreed that features of men or women can be arousing, and you cared for my lips, my shoulders, anything, odd as it may be, even my new walk, rising and dipping—*

I'm just going to repeat that part of the test, the responses weren't clear.

The library was shut for the week. The hospital receptionist suggested I enquire at the administration on the top floor. On I went. It was my mission. The lift again, no Ms Dorn this time. I knocked on the door of executive secretary Mrs J Rivers. Mrs J Rivers was in a big room with one other person, in the middle of a talk, but I will do what I can, she said. I wished more out of this meeting, more that I might somehow tell Ms Dorn and impress her with, but there was no more.

You will be glad to hear we can rule out a tumour. The MRI was blank. MRI is Magnetic Resonance Imaging. As of today, please note Ms Dorn, there will be less medication. Half-strength drip. And it would be good to change arms. I'll put in the new cannula—

Here, Dr Allen.

Excuse me if I look away.

Do that.

I looked Ms Dorn straight in the eyes. Blue, grey, the grey of what. Ms Dorn was the most beautiful woman ever. She looked straight at me, then at my arm. The needle may have gone in. I want a needle in my arm every day now, every hour.

There. Hold that pad there a moment.

I didn't feel a thing. Not as pain.

At night I reran this scene.

Here, Dr Allen.

Excuse me if I look away.

Do that.

I looked Ms Dorn straight in the eyes and smiled. She smiled. I smiled still. She smiled still. We smiled back and forth and back and forth.

Je t'aime.

I reran it to make my point with Teresa.

Here, the nurse said.

Excuse me if I look away, I said, and I looked the nurse straight in the eyes and smiled. She smiled. We smiled back and forth and back and forth.

Wow! said Teresa.

My question is, do you feel anything for any of the male nurses?

No, she giggled. I don't.

Not even Oscar?

God no.

I reran the optional version of the walk down the grey tunnel and the ten thousand pounds.

Ms Dorn said she would like to see me and insisted I took back the money. After seven weeks of dates she said she would like to sleep with me.

Ms Dorn was a martial arts expert but once we began living together she left the activity dormant, dividing her time instead solely between us and her career. For my part, I learned not to be squeamish before injured people. This took years.

I stayed in love with her. We had three children and three houses, one on the Mediterranean. In Nice, actually. We sometimes swapped it for an idyll in New England. All our children can ride horses.

Back from his pedicure, Malcolm retold his wartime tale, from when he was still Herr Gross, of the Russian village he quartered in as a teenage soldier and the Russian woman who one evening came dressed in a bearskin which she took off for the soldiers.

We were in the taiga, Malcolm said.

Like a jungle?

Malcolm ignored this question. He ignored all questions. He tried a new tale, of his stand-off with a caribou.

Fights were a common theme for Malcolm. Those stories always ended with a boot extinguishing something as if it was a cigarette on the ground.

A Plea For Eros pleads for classic feminism to be rolled up and put aside. Each sex may admit to being seduced by the other's lips, voice, hair. The sexes may stare at each other. Only once, briefly, have I noticed Ms Dorn's hair. So very slowly is my imaging moving across, I could be doing magnetic resonance imaging.

Malcolm's wife sat opposite me at the table.

The doctor said he might come out today. Now he's telling everybody he's coming out today. They won't stop him now. He has to use that whatchamacallit—that apparatus three times a day. It will go in the kitchen, we'll take out the microwave to make space for it. He'll have to stop smoking. But he won't. Once he starts he never stops anything.

Yes! said Malcolm coming in, beaming.

Ms Dorn swept in with a sheaf of papers.

This is a form for feedback from patients.

Like at a hotel.

This is not a hotel. It's anonymous and noncompulsory.

But I have no complaints. *Just desires.*

Take it or leave it.

I'll take it. Nothing is as seductive as a question, it's been said.

Many things have been said. Where is Mr Cross?

Getting his settings checked.

Where?

I don't know. But I'm glad we have a moment.

Don't imagine we have a moment. And psychotherapy is not included, it's an extra that isn't one of my tasks. Fill it in in your own time and give it to Oscar.

I'll come to the point. You're beautiful.

As that may be. You are rather ordinary-looking yourself.

Pretend I'm a top doctor.

You aren't.

Rich and famous. Rich or famous.

You aren't. You're just sick. You need to get your feet on the ground. Help me do that.

I am.

Ms Dorn?

What?

I can't find a place to say this on the form. But I'm glad we met.

Mrs J Rivers strode in to deliver the atlas in person. A lousy atlas, growled Malcolm, the health service is not what it was.

Giant Africa was shrunk to a double spread late on; but we pored over little Tunisia in the corner.

Don't go to Djerba, said Malcolm. There are more interesting places. Sousse, pearl of the Sahel.

His wife arrived with her sister and teenage family members.

Pearl of the Sahel, I'll say, she said. Is this box yours too?

Of course.

This bag? Then we'll carry all this down.

Malcolm feinted a punch in the stomach and touched me gently on the cheek with his other fist.

That's it, he said. *Mantelpiece*, he whispered. *Inside the sofa.*

Ms Dorn was in the corridor. Her hair was tawny and strong.

There you are, she said. I haven't seen enough of you out of your room. You aren't going to recover your balance unless you walk more. I want to see more of you out here.

She looked straight at me, in the eye.

I got the atlas. *I got the atlas, Mary.*

Good. The broccoli for us tonight?

I got the broccoli, plenty of it.

I know, Mrs Rivers was here in person. I'm glad. Are you satisfied now?

We found Tunisia. It was smaller than we would have liked. Have you been there?

No interrogations, please. That will be your last drip, by the way. Tomorrow, pills.

A strapping man on pills, it's ridiculous.

Ridiculous? You think I'm strapping? What does that mean?

I see a lot of you. You forget I see you every morning I'm on duty.

I don't forget. I can't wait for you.

She looked up and down the corridor, pushed me back into the room with the drip stands and the big sinks and the linen.

Quick, she said. Take off that stupid hospital shirt.

She unbuttoned the buttons.

It will have to be quick. Not my style but I can do it.

If someone comes?

You'd like that.

I—

They'll see, but they won't feel—what we'll feel. Lost your tongue have you, can't speak?

No. Yes.

Come on now. See my breasts. Still brown from the sun. Still salty from the water. I need the salt licked off.

The salt.

Pink pills. They'll be on your table when you wake up.

Night-time discoveries. If I lie close to the edge of the bed I go dizzy. If I move to the middle the dizziness stops. So my balancing mechanism keeps working at night (noticing one arm is not quite on the mattress). This is why we don't fall out of our beds. I will tell Ms Dorn. I want to see her reaction when I use the word *bed*.

I feel drowsy.

It is morning, said Ms Dorn thrusting back the cheap curtains. You are on the floor.

I know.

Since when have you been there?

Since recently.

Recently.

I don't think anything's broken.

You should not be on the floor. You should get up.

I've got my slippers on still.

People have stood up in slippers before.

Aren't you going to help?

All right. Sit up.

You're very strong.

I am. Now sit on the bed. Next time you consider lying on the floor let us know beforehand.

Send a postcard?

A postcard will be fine.

I dumped him, said Teresa. You know what he said? He said *How can you leave me just when you need me most?*

And you said?

That's crap, I told him. As if he was the only fish in the sea. Tomorrow I'm coming out to a brand new, wide-open world.

Dr Allen stood before his team.

You *will* recover your balance. First we will do two more tests. Another MRI, lower down the spine. The tests are not harmful or painful, but you need to sign your consent. Ms Dorn or I will answer any questions you may have. You will be out of here very soon. Then stay active. Don't work for a week. Don't climb ladders. See an ear doctor right away. Do you have any questions? In that case, Ms Dorn, can you get the papers ready?

They are ready, Dr Allen.

So. I have to go back to the unit.

Do you have something to sign with, no I see you don't. Here. Ms Dorn? *Mary?*

Yes?

I took the book back to the library.

You were expected to. Sign in that box at the bottom.

Our faces were very close. She didn't shrink back. *Beautiful.* Here?

There where my finger is.

The lines on her knuckles were beautiful.

Twenty thousand.

No.

So next week I will be out of the taiga. The jungle.

This is not jungle.

But it is raw.

Raw? It's eleven twenty-seven. I have work to do. I want to see you out in the corridor.

Mrs Harder took back the headphones. Now we will do a repeat MRI. In this cabin. *Only we don't need to repeat it. I just need to go into the cabin with you. Lie down.*

Mrs Harder—

A woman takes an average of twenty-seven minutes to reach an orgasm. A man eleven.

Do you have twenty-seven minutes?

I've been thinking hard about this moment. I don't need twenty-seven minutes.

Is this real?

This is real.

You're to go, tomorrow. Officially discharged.

You're so hard with me, Ms Dorn. There's something I'd like to say before your shift is over.

It is over.

You're going home now?

As it happens, yes.

Where is that?

Over there.

You live with Dr Allen.

No.

Will you have children with him?

That's not a question to put to a sister.

You aren't a sister. And you're off duty. *I'm in love with you.* I can imagine you with children. Children with ponies. What would their names be?

The children or the ponies?

Children.

How do I know? said Ms Dorn shrugging her shoulders very loosely and easily. Alice. Conrad. Polly.

Polly.

When you go, make sure you empty your cupboard.

I will, but I will be leaving with a problem.

You came in with one.

But there's no resolution. I thought you could help me.

I'm the last person to resolve things. It's your problem. Your solution.

I thought Ms Dorn, Mary, if you just weren't so hard on me, I might be attracted less. It's the hardness that draws me.

I like hardness. I like my man to be tough somehow.

Like a diver, an athlete, a rock-climber.

Why not. And what you need to do is get some of this yourself. Get strong again. At the moment you just aren't a match.

I'm not getting better. I could die.

I don't think so.

We both stared through the window. The sun was at its highest. Sister Sarah brought in lunch and went out.

So, said Ms Dorn, you'll have to work on yourself. You do have some strengths. A way with words. When you talk you can say something that lights everything up. At least that's what Teresa told me.

Teresa?

So you could work more on that. Goodbye. You may shake my hand.

Goodbye, Mary.

Goodbye.

Outside again. Snow's gone.

Ms Dorn gone, Mrs Harder, the doctors and nurses. Malcolm out there somewhere, reaching in his mantelpiece, telling tales.

It's windy. There are beds of plants pushed back stiffly, trees dancing, clouds with all their edges smudged. I will take a taxi—though would much like to walk down that bending street. I'll come back for that, when I have the strength.

Teresa is out there too, listening carefully to some new man. I hadn't noticed I could light everything up. I can work on that. That's what I'll be working on.

Printed in the United Kingdom
by Lightning Source UK Ltd.
120741UK00001B/112